WINNER of
the Guadalajara Book Fair
International Prize for Romance Languages (2021)

WINNER of
Chile's National Prize for Literature (2018)

WINNER of the Altazor Award
with the novel *Fuerzas especiales* [Special Forces] (2014)

Finalist of the Neustadt International Prize
for Literature (2012)

Finalist of the Rómulo Gallegos Prize
with the novel *Impuesto a la carne* [Meat Tax]
(2011)

WINNER of
the José Donoso Latin American Literature Prize
(2010)

WINNER of
the José Nuez Martín Prize
with the novel *Los vigilantes* [*Custody of the Eyes*] (1995)

WINN
Guggenheim F<

T0273043

# NEVER DID THE FIRE

First published by Charco Press 2021
Charco Press Ltd., Office 59, 44-46 Morningside Road,
Edinburgh EH10 4BF

A CIP catalogue record for this book is available from the British Library.

ISBN: 9781913867218
e-book: 9781913867225

www.charcopress.com

Edited by Bill Swainson
Cover designed by Pablo Font
Typeset by Laura Jones
Proofread by Fiona Mackintosh

Diamela Eltit

# NEVER DID THE FIRE

Translated by
Daniel Hahn

CHARCO PRESS

# FOREWORD

## by Julián Fuks

Can the subjugated speak? Can the oppressed speak? Can the disillusioned speak? Can the defeated speak? From out of the pages of this book, no exact answer to these questions will emerge. Within the pages of this book, the subjugated, the oppressed, the disillusioned, the defeated, all one voice, one single voice, speak. In the pages of this book, this subject, who is so often silenced, cannot but speak. Speak and, as far as possible, express the constant discomfort of the body, the meanness of successive days. To speak has become imperative. The final act of freedom in a world that wants them quiet, numbed, suppressed: finding words that will at last prevent them from not existing.

We are in an uncertain year, a year of dismay like so many others we have seen. In the year in question, one recollection recurs: the unpunished death of General Franco, the unseemly death of the fascist dictator untouched by any justice. Nothing to celebrate in that death, or in the insistent memory of the death: perhaps that's the greatest expression of the defeat of so many emancipatory struggles, the absurd triumph of the Spanish dictatorship, or of almost all dictatorships. In this uncertain year, already distant from that occurrence that's so real it becomes a symbol, there is no hope that might pay us a visit, no confidence that it could be possible to attain the slightest dignity, or at least an effective democracy.

We are once again shut up in a constrained space, inside a Beckettian room perhaps, the room from whose walls the same voice echoes incessantly. What's different, however, is the delirium, what's different is the madness that is ordered here – we are surrendered to the unending recollections of a life run through with politics. The experience of militancy becomes the centre of all memories, the many mistakes made during the resistance, mistakes that are re-enacted in the present, in the friction between bodies, in the non-viability of any real contact, of any understanding. Within the language, so intimate and so personal, of these bodies in conflict, the failure of direct action is made manifest, but another greater failure is made manifest too: the impossibility of reaching a more just, more human community, the evidence of a society condemned to perpetuate its violences. What's different is the continent, what's different is the time, is the historic trauma: we are in the very heart of the Latin American tragedy.

The voice that speaks to fill the silence, the voice that others want silenced, and it could not be otherwise, is the voice of a woman. The nameless narrator was unable to speak for decades – for centuries, for millennia, time here stretches out with no discernible limits – or at least she was unable to be heard, nobody wanted to hear her. No surprise that her tone now is burdened, at once, paradoxically, with pain and with indolence. This woman, too, is burdened, overburdened by a vast number of chores. Care for the man who oppressed her throughout her life, care for the child who is dying for all eternity, care for a whole multitude of decadent bodies.

She only cannot care for herself and for her own body, her fragmented body, deprived of the integrity it once had. Her body has been stormed by all society, her cells no longer belong to her, nor does the sweat belong to her that seeps from her pores in this constant drudgery. Her own time does not belong to her – all she has left is her voice, the possibility of doggedly questioning the past and, with words, occupying the present.

Why talk, what use is it now, reckon up the losses or reconstruct the defeat, the successive and unmistakable defeat?, asks the man who shares the bed with her, and the man who is writing these words asks it too, deferring her pages with this dispensable prologue. This woman has no reason to explain herself, and nor does Diamela Eltit have any need to explain herself, having written this full-powered novel. In this woman's voice, or in Diamela Eltit's, literature is transformed into a visceral, intimate speech, a speech that comes from inside the body and never surpasses it and yet which touches us all relentlessly. A literature of intervening in bodies and in times, a literature for disturbing the order of silences. Let this woman speak at last.

Julián Fuks
São Paulo, November 2019

*Never did the fire ever*
*play its part better as the dead cold*

César Vallejo

For Rubí Carreño.

With thanks at the time of this book to
Silviana Barroso, Francisco Rivas
and Randolph Pope.

W e are lying in the bed, surrendered to the legitimacy of a rest we deserve. We are, yes, lying in the night, sharing. I feel your body folded against my folded back. Perfect together. The curve is the shape that holds us best because we can harmonise and dissolve our differences. My stature and yours, the weight, the arrangement of bones, of mouths. The pillow supports our heads in balance, separates our breathings. I cough. I lift my head from the pillow and lean my elbow on the bed to cough more easily. It bothers you, my cough, and to some extent it worries you. Always. You move so as to let me know you're there and that I've overdone it. But now you sleep while I maintain my ritual of wakefulness and drowning. I'm going to have to tell you, tomorrow, yes, it really will be tomorrow that I'll need to cut back on your cigarettes, to ration them significantly or stop buying them altogether. We can't afford them. You'll clench your jaw and you'll close your eyes when you hear me and you won't answer me, I know it. You'll remain unmoved as if my words were totally unfounded and as if the pack I faithfully buy you was still there, full.

You like it, you think it's important, you need to smoke, I know this, but you can't do it any more, I can't, I don't want to. Not any more. You'll think, I know you will, about how you've kept yourself going on the cigarettes you systematically consume. That's how it has been, but it is no longer necessary.

No.

No, I can't sleep and in between the minutes, through the seconds that I cannot quantify, a worry inserts itself that is absurd but which declares itself decisive, the death, yes, the death of Franco. I can't remember when it was that Franco died. When it was, what year, what month, in what circumstances, you told me: Franco's died, he's finally died lying there like a dog. But you were smoking and so was I at the time. You were smoking as you talked about the death and I was smoking and while all my attention was on your teenage face, openly resentful and lucid and also dazzling in its way, I stubbed out my cigarette knowing it was the last, that I wouldn't smoke ever again, that I'd never really liked inhaling that smoke, and swallowing the burning of the paper. I feel your elbow resting against my rib, I think about how I still have my rib and I accept, yes, I surrender to your elbow and I resign myself to my rib.

I turn, put my hand on your hip and I shake you once, twice, fast, obvious. When did Franco die, I ask you, what year? What, you say, what? When did he die, I say, Franco, what year? In one movement you sit up in bed, quickly, filled with a muscular force you never exercise any more and which surprises me. You lean your head against the wall, but then immediately slip down between the sheets again to turn your back on me.

When, I ask you, when?

Your breathing agitated, you move towards the edge of the bed, I don't know, you answer me, be quiet, woman, turn over, go to sleep. A precise day of a precise year but which is no part of any order. A scene that's detached, inarticulate now, in which we were smoking, focused, so committed to that first cell of ours, while you, precociously wise, with all the fullness that talent can sometimes allow, you pronounced a few legitimate, coherent words that couldn't be ignored and we all looked enraptured at you – your arguments – as you explained the death of Franco and I, transfixed by the toughness of your words, put out my cigarette possessed by a final disgust and watched the paper crushed against the filter, looked at it in the ashtray and thought, never again, that's the last one, it's over, I thought and I thought why had I smoked so much that year if I didn't even like the smoke, not really. I can picture the ashtray, the stubbed-out cigarette with the scant strands of tobacco loose at its centre. I've got that. I've got Franco's death too, but not the year, nor the month let alone the day. Tell me, tell me, I ask you. Don't start, don't keep on, go to sleep, you answer. But I can't, I don't know how to sleep without first retrieving the lost plot, without dodging the terrible blank in time that I need to draw to me. The cigarette butt crushed against the ashtray, my fingers, the sequence of your convincing words, lying there like a dog, in his bed, the killer or maybe you said: the murderer and my final disgust at the mouthful of smoke, the last one.

The public death of Franco, lying in bed, dying of everything, with practically no organs, you said, the tyrant, you were saying, dead of old or very old age, surrounded by his entourage, you were saying, by Francoists, doctors. At night, late, on the edge of an exhausting dawn, the discussions, the arguments continued, and among all the possible words, of course, yours were the ones that sounded most expert or most accurate, while I smoked right through that unwavering night until, all of a sudden, I felt truly acidic, in my lungs, and I had to put it out, the cigarette, for ever.

Then you offered me one, want a cigarette?, day was already breaking, no, I don't. No, I said, I don't want one, and I glimpsed in your eyes a flicker of concern mixed with an obvious disappointment. A first, nascent, unforgivable look of abandonment or of a material grudge. But tell me, when. Shut up. You shut me up at the exact moment the calamitous bedsheet became entangled, once again, in my legs and my arms, just sit up, move, while I arrange the sheet, furious, not understanding if my fury's towards me or towards you, unconvinced. How could I have forgotten the year, a year you remember but won't tell me, to prevent me from settling the matter of the cigarette.

Stalinist, Martín called me, later, many years on, at a time in which we no longer were (at this very moment Martín steps forward, he's standing at the foot of our bed, out of place, denying my words, reiterating his lies in this century). He called me a Stalinist and you, listening to his words, hearing them, you turned your head, impassive as if he never had. Who was it called me a Stalinist, shut up. Who was it, I insist, shaking your hip. Oh, you say to me, I need to sleep, go on, sleep, please sleep, leave me in peace. You've raised your voice, you're speaking to me in a tone that's wild. Aggressive.

My eyes are burning from a dream that seems no more than a symptom. I can't sleep, shut up. Stalinist, he skewered me with the word just like that, while I looked at you seeking your defence and you, already settled into indifference, remained apart, while I listened to words that spun madly without completely understanding the rage that was generating them. Stalinist, he called me. He repeated it. I do know who said it, Martín (from the edge of the bed he touches his head, he shows off, displays his outline that is visibly irregular, eroded). In my retina I hold his eyes and all the nuances of their expression, but now I'm waiting for you to be the one to say who it was, waiting to hear as much from your lips, from yours, why did you say nothing, what degree of desertion had you reached, quite unruffled, I remember it.

4

It doesn't matter, you say to me, go to sleep, let it go, forget about it.

In the middle of an argument that seemed ridiculous, when everything had already become muddled, you had shown up just to listen ambiguously, marking your distance and your irony and I couldn't, I wasn't able to keep silent, I couldn't manage it and I said, how come, and I said, seems unfair or inappropriate if you ask me, I managed to say both things or perhaps, perhaps I expressed, with a discomfort that had been soothed, I know it, that it was impossible to have a conversation in those terms and that was when the final condemnation was triggered, connected to a concise response: Stalinist. Move your leg, it's bothering me, your trousers are scratching me, why do you have to sleep with your trousers on. Shut up.

But now dawn is going to break again. I know that afterwards we never mentioned what had happened, and we wielded a disproportionate politeness. We did it as we turned away from what was to be the final meeting of that cell. Yes. You behaved as though I deserved all deference, as if it were possible to believe that nothing had happened. But it was the final meeting of an intransigent year that none of the words you used could contain any longer.

You behaved like a dog.

You had already been transformed into a dog, I think now. I think this while my arm in its surrender to wakefulness tortures me with its unavoidable rubbing against the monolithic wall that surrounds us.

It was more than a hundred years ago that Franco died. The tyrant. Profoundly historical, Franco plundered, occupied, controlled. He was, of course, consistent with the part he had to play. One of the best actors for considering his period. An old man. A soldier. Decorated by the institutions. Not brilliant, no, never that, but effective, stubborn, neutral. Foolish, you say, he was foolish. A whole century's gone by now. No, no, you tell me, not a century, it's more than that, much more. Yes, I answer you, everything moves in a certain way, imprecise, never literal, not ever. We are talking a century later – more than a century – we are calmly exchanging words that are friendly and compassionate. We need to guard against the scream that we never allow ourselves, not ever, because we might injure ourselves and break. You don't shout at me and nor do you assume overly disdainful expressions, you skip them and just let them circulate inside your head. My own determination is focused on controlling any glimmer of bitterness in order to be a part of this peace we have granted ourselves. We are in a state of peace that is something close to harmony, you curled up into a ball in the bed, covered by the blanket, your eyes closed or half-open, me on the chair, parsimoniously and lucidly ordering the numbers that sustain us. A column of numbers that accounts for the strict diet to which we are subjected, a routine and efficient nutrition that goes directly to meeting the demands of each of the organs that govern us.

We eat precisely. Briefly.

Rice is related to bread, both fulfilling their role of providing us with sleep and relief. We eat bread and rice. I always prepare the rice the same way. The rice, its common form, the necessary cooking that does require a certain concentration, it's bad, the rice is bad, when it ends up overcooked or almost raw, its repulsive grains that more than once have gone down the wrong way. Yes, you cough and the grains come out of your mouth until they're tumbling chaotically on the blanket, propelled by your blocked throat, and oh you're choking, you could die, how painful this rice cough is and the saliva you spit along with the grains disturbs me. I don't want to look at the saliva mixed with the rice, resembling a light vomit or some watery substance, an impossible mess of nourishment that spatters and stains the bed you're occupying, my bed.

You smoke, and you eat.

And so you swallow the wrong way or you choke or you die. You smoke and you eat with the very same anxiety. I prefer not to say to you in this century: don't smoke. I give up on saying to you: don't smoke while you're eating, or saying, slowly, slowly so you don't choke, or saying, don't eat because it'll go down the wrong way, or saying, don't cough because that cough disgusts me and that tiny bit of vomit disgusts me, or saying, what's up, what's up with you and the rice, you look like a toothless kid or you look like a sick dog. I don't say anything so as to preserve the listlessness that this century grants us, a gift that cannot be refused, and that's why we can use Franco to attenuate: his fascism. No, you say, a Nazi. Fine, fine, I reply. It's not the same, you say, getting the concepts mixed up can lead to tragic consequences, don't you see? You say fascist with a lightness we really need to reconsider. Yes, I reply, employing a tone that seeks to be conciliatory, sometimes I do get mixed up. You don't get mixed up, no, that's not it, it's that you don't differentiate a fascist from a Nazi. Let's see, you say to me, what was Franco, which trend do you locate him in, how do you catalogue him, according to which parameters could you classify him, what was his structure really, how might one establish a hierarchy for reckoning with the things he did, which elements determine his affiliation, what was the paradigm that mobilised him, his policies, his strategies, the intractable bureaucracy he managed to establish.

He does maintain a surprising correlation with fascism, I say to you. He does it through his deceptively unilateral will, through that iconographic precision, through his solitude without the least trace of deviation. Through his death that was so pragmatic and universal. Through the embellishments of his parades, the troops, the distribution of power, the betrayal of his collaborators, the insatiable quest for legitimacy, through his wicked features, through the rictus sneer of his mouth, through his puny stature, through his strategies and his failures to understand when confronted with history, through his unhealthy attachment to his family, the ludicrous attitude of his wife and the avid fervour of his children. Did he have children, and how many? Don't avoid the subject, you say, don't seek refuge in details. Yes, that's right, we ought to be precise and complete.

More than a century has passed – do you realise that? – I say to you, an entire, broken century, a thousand years, a time that ends almost with no echo, as if it had never happened – do you realise that? With no ending and already it's memory. I know my statement might worry you or might bore you with the wake of banality it leaves behind, and so I get up from the chair, go to the kitchen and while I dig around in the pot, I experience a sort of vertigo, the faint inkling of a sickness that doesn't go so far as to worry me because I attribute it to the rice, to the multiplication of the grains that go round and round while a hasty reheating occurs. They jump about, mingle, they stick to one another, those grains, the rice that maintains us and strengthens us. I remove a portion and set it on the plate. I return to the bedroom and inform you, my tone overly enthusiastic, that it's time, you've got to feed yourself. I hold out the rice, you sit up a bit, tired, with a seriousness that concerns me. You eat half-sitting on the bed. I watch you, distracted, at a ceremony that has become natural. I remember how back in the century that, in a way, belonged to us, I used to watch your opining about the act of feeding with astonishment. I'd never thought of hunger as a dangerous act that required an underhand strategy to lessen it, until you told me, you pointed out that it seemed too personal to you, 'The act of eating is personal' and for that reason you asked me, with a caution that sought to not be harmful, not to look at you while you ate. You added, your tone pleasant and incidental, that if I kept doing it, you would move further away, that you preferred to be alone: I prefer to be alone, isolated with my food. You never used to look at me, it's true, when I was – and you pointed this out to me too – swallowing. You used that word. Swallowing, you said, and the insatiability contained in that verb made me despise it. I understood that my way of dealing with hunger was intolerable to you. What did we used to eat?, I ask myself now, before the rice, before getting into this craze for those grains. You did, I know, have a certain well-established aversion to dairy; to milk and its by-products. I laughed as you held up the piece of cheese, you were vacillating there, wondering whether it was adequate or, perhaps, whether it was indispensable. You remained engrossed. You looked entranced or terrified at the piece of cheese you held in your fingers. Your slim fingers, protected by the correctness of your bones and your short, neat nails and the moment when you pressed it between your fingers and pierced it with your nails. We saw how the cheese came apart, its shape, and the whole cell, the nine of us who made it up, couldn't help but exchange glances that were astonished yet shy, struck by the terrible way you squeezed.

Not cheese, not dairy.

We could eat only what was strictly necessary to our ends. It wouldn't do, that was how you put it, to surrender to food, turning it into a place that ended up obscuring the impact of hunger. Hunger had a function for you, I know. Hunger, you proclaimed as much, was a state that deepened rigour and allowed us to do concrete and sustained work. But oh, never satiety, no, not that, you insisted, because that would channel a drowsiness that obliged us to postpone our purpose. You hated drowsiness, you preferred, even in its discomfort, hunger. I would confirm this for myself, I did it when I surrendered myself to the glorification of foodstuffs, to their fatty excess. You hated it, fat, the fatty body and its shine. A body rounded by layers of a liquefied fattiness that produced the listlessness that deferred agility, that agility you demanded of the cell and which, if it was not up to your expectations, we would have to re-make with other bodies that were hungry and energetic. I look at you in the bed, I see you determined to dislodge the hunger, the first, obvious hunger that assails you. You eat uncensored, in a way I cannot but find uncomfortable. You would say, if you had any toughness left, that hunger could never be sated with rice because you're only complying with a simple demand from the organism, yours, from your particular organism, but you are not granting it the fat that is, in your opinion, the only substance that brings fulfilment and satisfaction.

I understand you.

I know the argument you make is impeccable, coherent, but all the same I'm distraught at the way you eat, hunched over the plate, using the fork to pick up, carelessly, the grains that jump from your mouth onto the bed or slip down off your lip or fall onto the edges of the plate or slide between your fingers. It's the fork, I think, its thin metallic shape, intensified by your position on the bed. But all the same, despite the fact I understand the context in which your plate of rice is dispatched, I cannot avoid what is intolerable. It is here, the explosive feeling of being present at a scene that is beyond my imagination and my possibilities. Don't look at me, you say, turn away. I do. I look at the floor and then at the notebook. I pick up the pencil and write down the last numbers, no, not really the last ones, but these provisional ones, those numbers in which we order ourselves. I wait. I'm waiting for you to finish your plate as I draw the number, I notice it, and when I hear you coughing and feel the heavy tobacco smoke flooding the room, I get up to retrieve the plate, gather up the grains and smooth out the bedspread.

I return to the table and to my chair. I forget, yes, I try to forget my fingers on the rice, gathering up the damp grains, I wipe my fingers on my skirt and then, decisively, I shut the notebook. I go over to the bed, sit on the edge, and wait to begin a peaceful exchange with you that will allow me to order some of the images that hover about me, images that are obsolete and come from a century whose end still rings out but prompts no emotion.

I step back.

It was more than a century ago, I say, a thousand years at least, that I was haunted by the dissonance of a phrase, the same phrase I noted down when captivated by the perfection of its design. However, I go on, it had an ambiguity to it, what ambiguity, you ask me, which one, listen carefully, I say: 'The working-men have no homeland. We cannot take from them what they have not got.' Ah, you say, no more, no more, how much longer, you murmur and raise your voice to say, why don't you bring me a cup of tea, I'm thirsty, I want some tea, a cup, you say to me.

I go to the kitchen. I wait patiently for the kettle to boil. I know it's going to rain tonight, the sky's too over-cast, I was expecting it. It will be cold tomorrow, when I go out onto the street, when I reach the stop, when I take the bus, when my legs hurt from the blocks I'll have to walk. Yes, it will be cold when I turn back and retrace my route. And I will be icy-cold still when I come into the room and find you lying on the bed and go into the kitchen to make myself a cup of tea, the same tea I bring to you in the bedroom and leave on the nightstand.

It's going to rain, I say.

There's no ambiguity, you say. The line is direct, real, understandable, correct. It's deceptive, I say. Explain. I don't want to; the journey to the kitchen, the possibility of rain, the steam from the tea, they cause a surprising slackness in me, I want to stretch out on my piece of bed, climb up and lie on my side and feel I have a body, that my legs and my arms are still around me and I'm not just some aching or tired or swollen kidneys, erasing me from myself. It's deceptive, I say to you, that line, it allows for too many interpretations, it uses the word homeland and that opens up an edge that's dangerously sentimental, crooked, in so far as it acknowledges it, that homeland, I say.

Ah, you say, ah.

But this is a day from a different century, from an age without distinguishing marks, a century that does not belong to us and which, nevertheless, we are compelled to experience and in this century everything seems unreal or expendable, yes, expendable. No, you say to me, that's not what it's like, you know that already, we analysed it, we were committed to measuring the effect of each word, we did it exhaustively until the cell understood, became expert, irreproachable, organic. Which cell?, I ask you, confused, which of all the various cells? You open your eyes. You have your eyes open and your back dangerously curved, does it hurt, I ask you, your back, does it still hurt? Yes, it does. What else hurts, tell me. My knees, one of my elbows, my stomach. Your bowels?, I ask you. No, no, my gallbladder. I didn't know, you never told me. It hurts me. I'm not worried about your bones, ultimately they're condemned in advance, what I care about, as you well know, are your organs, exposed and eager and fearsome. You said gallbladder just to punish me, because you know as well as I do that the supposedly perfect sentence did actually lend itself to slipping into what we so feared, into a reformism that could destroy the portents of a century that had ended mostly unremarked, and unremarkable, yes, especially that, caught in its own conformism, even you, who seemed incorruptible, you had to give in, you know, you gave in, you surrendered to the delusions that the century kept on producing to wear itself down. You did it and then broke the harmony of the most perfect and effective cell we had achieved. I don't say this to you, I think it. Franco was a fascist, right? Yes, he was. Why? For his inclination towards mass rallies and his vocation for stagecraft. For his sustained practices that just got sharper and sharper until they were verging on paroxysm. Was he a Nazi or was he not? Any answer is possible now that the century, those thousand years have concluded, it's mere speculation now, a predictable accumulation of useless conjectures. I'm going to lie down, I say.

No, you reply. Not yet, you insist. It's not time yet.

Stalinist, extremist, crazy killer bitch. One word after another, a group of words, developed into a relentless equation. Resonant, perfect syllables, organising a harmonic chain that rang out like a recurring litany. But something in that singular mechanism captivated me or distracted me and it's possible my face remained inclined towards these words or alert to them, it's possible, yes, that nothing in my face acknowledged the insult. And it's not strange that this exact expression, my own, should have conferred an impressive distance on me. I think it now, uncertain, unsure and I'd like to ask you whether by any chance, amid the chaos, my expression really had managed to win me such unusual exoneration. Perhaps I imagined it, thinking about those uncertain afternoons, hours, days when the fear of a resounding voice, yes a resounding voice, was able to intercept me, piercing me through with a sum total of words that might or not have meaning and that, nevertheless, could destroy. Or perhaps I was the one who was preparing myself for that moment, I myself the one who repeated what they were going to say, what could be made out, left, right and centre. The one who passed judgment. What you didn't want to hear. You no longer felt. It's possible. The facts crowd together and confuse me.

It's hard for me, yes, so hard.

Stalinist, extremist, crazy killer bitch.

The meeting had been difficult but not useless. You lost, yes, you lost the control that your positions had attained, you were brought down by your opponents' arguments. I was in agreement with the dominant group, I had colluded with the arguments you didn't share because they were, as you put it, unconducive. I registered that word, I'd heard that 'unconducive' of yours many times and I knew it was a trap, a word you put forward whose sole purpose was to obstruct. I knew I needed to take a stand against it. I did so perhaps too vehemently, with a hint, in a way, of hysteria or haste or eagerness that troubled even me. It was the tone that bothered me, not my decision to bring that word down. I needed to cancel it, its authority, the forced legitimacy you imprinted on it. A mask word that intimidated. Of course, I couldn't confront your assumptions directly. I drew my own conclusion, I held on to the simpler terms to distance myself from that habit of yours, that obsession with leaning on a density you employed to dramatise each one of your interventions. Finally, I submitted to the group that sought the end of a purposeless tyranny. A lucid group that had understood how much we formed a cell that seemed to have been constructed for you. I know that although this was not acknowledged, my intervention proved critical. I talked about direct actions although I didn't want to specify, there was no need. And so I interrupted the great volume of reformist ideas with which you sought to keep us captive. We need to analyse, you said, to analyse. With no need to state it explicitly, I opposed your proposal, I leaned towards direct action. I had already calmed down when I managed to take possession of the term 'direct action'.

I understood that I was entering the territory of a simple opposition, and that there you'd be able to defeat me with uncommon ease. And yet you didn't. You didn't want to expose me, or didn't want to expose yourself, I don't know, the truth is I still don't know even now. What does it matter. But that was the day, the hour, the moment when your defeat was written, the end of your empire, a delicate castle that you had erected for your own glory, a castle, something like a kind of deck of cards spread out in the middle of danger and possibly horror. I was able, once you had refused to intervene, to put my stamp on the course of the meeting, I did that, even though the voice of your ally, the most unconditional ally you had, one of your people, called me, driven by a scandalous disappointment, extremist and also called me, in an all too predictable outburst, Stalinist. Even amid these words that were meant to sow reproach and division, the cell agreed with me. Equipped with a careful strategy, I slipped away from the final discussions, I never once looked at you during the course of the final discussions, I remained on a more than discreet second or third plane, not any plane in reality, I withdrew as if I wasn't there, as if I had never spoken. I remained seemingly outside as your fate was sealed.

It was necessary, absolutely necessary.

Absolutely necessary to behead you because those ideas of yours, no, no, they meant no more than mere bureaucracy in the midst of a situation that seemed inexorable. We had become a cell with no purpose, lost, disconnected, loosely led by a group of words that were well-chosen and convincing words but stripped of reality. I know it was a tragic day for your comfortable expectations, but it couldn't or shouldn't have gone any differently. You no longer were. You had transformed into the most useful piece for confirming a catastrophe. You don't forgive me, I say to you in the middle of the night, I've repeated it to you on some of the most hopeless nights, you don't forgive me, do you? How much longer, you reply, let me sleep.

Yes, that exact night marked the course of what was to be our own life, that of the two of us. The precise life after we detached ourselves from that cell. But even though time doesn't stop flowing, not ever, still we live like militants, austere and focused on our principles. We think like militants. We're convinced our ethics are the only appropriate ones. We know this, we establish this at every moment. We understand that we cannot allow ourselves to be subjugated to common feelings, we know that history will end up on our side. We need no confirmation, we don't even need to discuss it within the cell into which we have transformed ourselves. We are a cell, a single clandestine cell cloistered in this room, with a controlled, careful exit to the kitchen or the bathroom. You're still at the head, you steer. I try to obey. I make an effort to achieve total loyalty. I do it with the conviction that, yes, now your leadership really is profound and correct. You were able to polish up your leadership after rigorously measuring the use of each of your words. You set overblown terms to one side. When did you do it, in which minute did you abandon those pompous words, when was it?

We would say in unison, I'm sure, that it happened after that uncontrollable volume of words entered a state of calm, when that deeply cellular, minuscule moment was unleashed. The silence, yours, ours, a larval silence that waits, that waits, that gives itself up faithfully to time, because now we are word bodies, word, yes, bodies. We could capitulate, but we no longer want to or know how to capitulate, how to do it, to whom we should give ourselves up, or what to give up of ourselves, to whom we should hand over our arsenal of experiences and extensively cultivated practices. What punishment or reward would apply to us for our actions. We no longer know how to capitulate.

I honestly don't know. Nor do you.

You lie to me. Often. It's a very well-known mechanism, a disorienting technique we depend upon. We need to move about, to amplify this time in the same way your leg stretches out on the bed, painful, stiff, closed in by the inescapable effects of arthritis. Does it hurt, I ask you, a lot, your leg. No, you say, what does it matter to you. But tell me, tell me, it does hurt, what do you care, it's my affair, mine, the pain, my leg. Just so.

Yes. Just so. You are at each moment more precise despite the night being decisive for our ends. You murmur at night. You know it, I've told you: 'you talk during the night'. You do it because you cannot control yourself, you just don't know how to keep quiet. Shut up, I say. And you do. For a reasonable stretch of time, but you start up again driven by certain orders that you impose upon yourself. I cover my head with a pillow. I don't want to hear one word, not one more. My work is done, I don't need to hear you, I don't want to know. I shouldn't. They're intimate words of which I cannot be a part, I put the pillow over my head and I'm not even bothered by the slight breathlessness it provokes in me. A flimsy, worn, old thing, that's what it is, the pillow is old and I ought to replace it. One for me and another for you. That would be fair, it would be the right thing. I cover my head so as to be able to sleep, but of course, it's not possible, in reality, it's not physical. I do, sooner or later, need air. I remove the pillow from my face and what I see, with a nonsensical logic, is how we were leaving that other room. Bit by bit the meeting's intensity decreased until complete discomfort was produced, the most absolute of all.

Poblete prepared to act against me, he did it expertly. And he did, of course, have the necessary ability. He was extraordinarily sharp, a verbose craftsman who took refuge

19

on the edge of a word, on the threshold of an expression with no content, simply a marginal note that stemmed the flows, my flow, and which he began systematically to exert without giving me any respite. Later on, as was logical, his frontal attacks would begin, quick and decisive. Poblete, and history has shown this to be so, was more than usually skilled, a master in the function of making himself visible without any great fuss. You see, I say to you, what Poblete's doing, the whole time. No, no, no, you say, what do you care, I don't care, I don't care at all, you say with a groan.

You want me to raise your leg, I say, I'll rub it for you, take your trousers off, no, no, no, you say, bring me water, I'm just thirsty, but don't turn on the light, you say. Please don't turn it on, you repeat.

At one specific moment of the night I felt contaminated by your weight. That moment of the night weighed on me and I knew it was you, I knew it was your weight collapsing on top of the night. You fell. You disintegrated into a thousand pieces. I understood, I could see that you were on your way out, that you intended for me to support you both, the night and you. You didn't care at all about my effort. Not even a bit. You'd decided. You decided it long before surrendering to the habit of monosyllables.

It's alright, it was necessary.

No, it wasn't necessary, it was a mere subterfuge, mine, yours. We're going blind, I want to say, almost blind. Our sight. What, what?, don't talk any more, keep quiet. Yes, that's true, you're totally, totally right, we ought to keep quiet, we need to follow the rigid path to which we've committed ourselves. No matter that dawn will soon be breaking, that's going to happen anyway, it's too predictable and independent an act, incredibly universal, so much so that it's no longer even moving. You are, you said, not very industrially minded. What?, I answered, what are you saying?, should I be?, should I be?, I asked because I needed you to guide me, to lead me towards this precise course. Help me to be industrial I wanted to say, help me, but I couldn't, oh yes, you answered, you should be, but you're not. You no longer were. What, I wanted to say, what are you talking about, you're not industrial either. Yes, I am, you answered, my brain. In my teenage years I couldn't fight it off, there was something stopping me, it was really a kind of indifference, a way of isolating myself perhaps or of being on my guard. You understood, that exact day, the day of your industrial accusation, that I was not really listening to you, not to anyone, ever, I never listened when people were accusing me, what I mean is it didn't affect me while it was happening, literally, it did later, for hours, days, years, the sounds and images, their concepts and implications remained on the cyclical outer edges of my thoughts, as if those words and those scenes belonged to me or were entirely mine, my sole creation.

For ever, incessantly cursing myself.

It'll be morning soon, I tell you, not long now. Yes, you say or I think you say. It'll be cold today, from now on it'll get colder every day, won't it? Yes, yes, you reply. Worn out by my words, you just murmur, yes, yes. Why am I even mentioning the weather. It's stupid. You don't go out on your own, not ever, unless it's strictly, very strictly necessary. That's how things ended up being stipulated. Don't go out, I said to you, it's not necessary, lie down. Cover yourself up, it's cold. We remain, to a great extent, clandestine, we position ourselves on the outside, radically. We don't depend on civilian names, we remain attached to our last aliases, we've already gotten used to them, or taken possession, I don't know. But if somebody were to say my civilian name, I wouldn't turn towards them. What for. You could be in the crosshairs, for sure, it would be you.

Don't go out, don't go out.

I pass unnoticed, my studied insignificance, that'll still be able to save us, oh no, no, never save us, even my deep opacity couldn't shield us. The light comes in cautiously, a light that is altogether blocked. The time is approaching. Yes, I remember telling you. We should make a decision.

I was crying because I was terrified, I knew what was going to happen. We must hurry, take him to the hospital. Either you take him or I will. No, no, no, it's impossible, impossible. Soon I'll be going out and it's overcast, with that grey that flattens the landscape, puts it on the level of an awkward realism, a landscape that just isn't worth it. Doesn't mean anything. The grey.

I've still got, what, how long left?, an hour, maybe a bit more, before I get up, have a cup of tea, go to the bathroom, get dressed, go out, board the bus, walk two or three blocks, even four. Go into the house, carry out my work diligently, collect my pay, come back, yes, come back in a light mist repeating the journey – the street, the bus, its rocking, the always difficult act of alighting, the blocks walked to reach the room and find you just as you are now, curled up, neither totally asleep nor awake, surrendered to that watchful drowsiness that transports you with equanimity from waking to sleep. I'll spend hours out, those hours of travelling, of the exact interior of that house, yet when I return to the room, when I see you in the bed it will look, I know, like an unchangeable scene and I will no longer be able to understand where the line that governs time is exactly. I lived, yes, amid a very fine perceptual disturbance. Incredibly, and in a way that's hard to express, I suffered that cancelling of time. On a day in that other century, in other centuries, a time when I walked and walked, but could not move forward. I didn't advance a single millimetre because I always stalled on an identical perimeter of the block. I ended up being assailed by an inexpressible confusion of time, while you lay there completely safe in the room, stretched out on the bed, protected by the worn old blanket. I was the one who went out, as we had agreed, but my senses were chaotic. We must forget the horror of that night. What could have happened?, I ask you now that dawn's about to break. I don't finish the phrase, I never do, because you lose your temper or you block your ears or, if you're up to it, if your muscles permit, you get up and shut yourself in the bathroom. Or else in the middle of the night or at its start, on one of the compulsory turns in bed, when we're face to face, without seeing each other, sensing each other in the night, I say to you, why didn't we take him, I ask you, seriously why didn't we take him to hospital?

Ah, ah, you murmur.

And I'm not sure if that's a moan or a lament coming out of your mouth and you turn as quickly as your body allows and move violently, compelling me to reposition myself on the narrow ruined mattress that abuses our bones. A perceptual disturbance that is fine but also familiar, a basic sign of tiredness or a tiny attack on my mental fortitude linked to my exhaustion. A state that became abruptly evident as I walked, destroyed, while thinking, indelibly, about the last scenes, that little two-year-old face and his anguished grimace of death. Suddenly, the image was intercepted by an unusual impression. I wasn't moving forward at all. The physical reality of this street in the city had stopped. I alone was moving in a unique setting that didn't stop happening. It was simply occurring beyond what I understood could possibly be real and, nevertheless, the concreteness of the situation forced it onto me. I shut my eyes, tried to stop or to breathe or to lean against the wall. Time was hurling itself forward, all possible time was there, material and non-transferable. And I myself didn't count, I was merely a body trapped in a space that was in turn controlled by time. Later I was able to understand that it was only a bad experience, a trap opened by the fury of the senses. I couldn't tell whether it was a privilege or the edge of a nightmare. I was walking but not advancing, I couldn't advance, I tell you. You don't answer. Something physical happened, something scientific, I say, because time and space, I manage to say before you move and I understand that you don't want to hear because you've covered your head with the pillow, you're the one who's done it this time and the pillow over your face is so solid that I am assailed not by rage, no, but by resignation, that feeling I know so well and which, somehow, ends up being effective.

Resignation.

To what? I just resign myself. I should wait an hour. The light is beginning to show itself, fleetingly. In an hour I will cross the little bed taking care not to fall, I mustn't, I mustn't fall and I don't want to crush your legs while I slide down the bed. I mustn't do it because they hurt, they do, so much, your legs, your knees, your ankles and hips, you say, they hurt, your bones hurt, I know, much more than you're willing to admit. I can tell from the way you move about, ever skinnier, coiled in on yourself, that edginess caused by the pain. But the painkillers are working for you, they still manage to take some of the edge off. Take, I say, two pills, only two, because any more will mess up your stomach, did you hear me?, I say. You move in the bed trying to slip away. Answer me, I insist, only two. And don't spill your tea on the sheets, don't forget to turn off the fire on the stove if you go to the kitchen, don't go leaving the flame on, listen to me, the stove, you will turn it off, stay in bed, I say, don't get up, it's cold, have your tea, don't knock it over, don't stain the sheet, don't wet the blanket, I'm leaving the coat here for you, on the chair, you see it?, for when you go to the bathroom, I tell you, put on the coat, don't catch a cold. Two pills, did you hear?, just two. I stop in the doorway. I see you swollen in the bed. What do I see? A curled-up lump, you, dislodging the body you used to have so as to allow the arrival of what has now appropriated you. I see the lump that contains you, the same one that compels you and I confirm how used I've become to that shape, it's already imprinted on my retina, that lump belongs to me, yours, and I find it hard, almost impossible to go back, to find you on your feet, upright, with your eyes so bright and alive, those eyes that set you apart or your countenance that's now lost. You had a body that while never vigorous did have something unique about it. If I close my eyes I can see you, your body but perhaps it's an invention or a false image that never quite belonged to you. Standing against the light, voice numbed by anxiety, with your whole young body frozen stiff with pain you told me that the entire party leadership had fallen. The best we had. As evening drew in. You were framed in the theatrical effects of the dazzling twilight that radiated from the window. No, I said to you, no. All of them?, I asked. Yes, all of them. Or else you sit and read, yes, you read, with a remarkable focus that captivates me, you read amid the difficulty caused by the inadequate size of the print. You read without seeing. What was your face like? I try to recompose it but all I can see is the lump tangled among the disordered blankets and the edges of bedsheets coming out of the sides, a face that's blank, oh no, no. I could reconstruct the face we had, because we did have a face and, yes, bodies too. Both of us, always. We'd walk with an almost excessive share of energy along streets, looking for our early cell, looking for it because we'd convinced ourselves it was the only possibility, the one thing that could contain us in history, in this story, we'd say, that was still active and we'd say: never above us, never governing us with its monstrous assumptions, we were awaiting history's inescapable arrival. There was a face and a body, there were expressions on the face and the bones, bones with no hierarchy, consigned to

26

mere existence, practically with no place, bones that are elastic, even flexible, that allowed you to do that impressive bending over till you touched the floor. You enjoyed doubling over like a contortionist. No, you didn't enjoy it, it was just an exercise or a test, a game no doubt in which I was compelled to follow you. I was able, too, bending over, to put my hands, my palms, I mean, on the ground. Stay in that position for some moments. Many. I don't know what induced us to adopt these childish shapes. Now I shake my head and reproach myself.

How could we have surrendered ourselves to these meaningless acts?

Or how did we allow our time to be spent playing cards. Playing to beat each other, according to the strategies that the rules of the game offered us. How could we recognise, without being ashamed, that we liked to play card games, that we did it when there were hours to kill, yes, playing over and over, surrendered compulsively to a fervour that was so, so banal. Your nimble hands flourishing the fan of cards, shuffling them, waiting with disproportionate longing for the luck that the pack would bring us, your misfortune when you lost.

You lost and you couldn't conceal your displeasure.

Or perhaps it was my immoderate winner's pride that ended up afflicting you, my laughter at your losing, all those points that counted against you and you'd end up so sullen. I can clearly see how in those moments that already seem timeless there was no way for you to recognise that you were upset, grieving at having lost, wounded.

Stupid parlour games, inoffensive but totally backward. I said this to you. We can't and we shouldn't. That's what I told you, we can't play, we shouldn't, not any more. You complied. Meanwhile, perhaps as a kind of revenge, you refused to dance. I enjoyed it, I must admit, that kind of happiness or autonomous energy woven between music and dancing. That entirely corporeal aspect which in a way expressed the syntax of a body that is nothing but itself. But if I did it, if I gave in to the music, if I surrendered to the dancing, your disgruntled look would prevent me from concentrating, would make me lose the necessary harmony I was supposed to preserve with my partner. I turned clumsy, ridiculous. You managed to make me not dance. Neither one of us did. But today I want to ask you – I'm going to do it tonight – what you felt when you danced with her. If the two of you ever did it, if you had the chance to embrace in the middle of a dance, if you embraced while dancing, if you enjoyed dancing with her. If you danced. I need to do it, it's a still outstanding question I need to resolve and you will answer me this time, although you are a lump in the bed, you'll have to tell me what you did, what was the quality of the fun, at what point the laughter was unleashed, that terrible complicity that is caused by such mirth, why you were laughing, I saw you, I know, like the most reliable witness, that you did it, it's just that now I can't see the gleam of your teeth or even the enchanted, captivated expression that accompanied your laughter, much less remember her face at that moment, the same face that allowed me to guess that I was outside and that I needed, it was my duty, to understand it, to accept a decision I had no part in. I'm going to ask you a series of linked, precise questions, whether you danced, when you did it, where and I'll ask you how the decision was taken, what arguments were put forward and what you did with your guilt. I won't accept your refusal, I will not allow it. I look at you from the edge of the bed and I hesitate. No, no, no. Not even a dog deserves that, I think, what's the point.

Yes. After a thousand years, what's the point?

No.

The two of you were chatting and laughing. I know I was assailed by a profound unease, I also know that I moved forward impulsively, that I intervened, it was imperative that I intervene: we've got to go. I was clearly challenging you, it's time. No, you answered, not yet. Yes, I insisted, in what at this precise moment seems a ridiculous attitude. No. The tone in which you said it was too definitive. Blunt. There was nothing for me to do but leave, go, across the room filled with bodies, exposing myself to people's eyes and then disappearing, to be lost to them, to the two of you. A progressive emotion was being unleashed, beyond my control. Yes, emotion. I was feeling with astonishing emphasis. I was being increasingly eaten away by an adverse and yet extraordinary outer crust of feelings. They astonished me, my feelings: negative, intense and suffering. So much so that I didn't fit there, my consciousness, until I was transformed into something like a bright beam that expelled me from myself and simultaneously held me back at an unreal limit about to be breached, shattered against a humiliating and radical solitude, pushed into the experience of such an internal and unclassifiable process where hatred seemed material and embedded in the impossibility of giving it some route, some way out, some vent for dismantling the hatred, a viral trace to disseminate it and dislodge it, the sickness, the hatred, I mean, mine, whose strength in me even I did not know.

Pure hatred.

Why did I think you were dancing?, no, you weren't dancing, no, you were talking in a way that was extraordinarily intimate, that's what I'm thinking now, yes, both bodies were occupying the words like a kind of simple subterfuge. There you were, apart, falling to pieces, a common man. Fragile and common. I notice how pale you are. Did you eat, I say, did you eat the rice I left you. Yes, yes. I wish I were back there, for all those hours to go past again in all their excess, yes, returning to precisely the same point, my look, the night, identical space, the contempt and the humiliation you subjected me to, I'd like to see, smell, suffer that situation to lose myself to myself. Those were hours of a marvellous fullness, that brazenness, mine. Does your head hurt?, I ask. I deduce it, I guess it from the way you bring your hands to your temple. The migraine that occasionally disables you. I watch your migraine-stricken, dark expression, the years of our faces. We have lost it, our face, time has transformed us into human forms that are radically mass-produced, serial, but provided with a rigour, that opaque and disciplined series in which a militant is recognised, a true militant, like us who faithfully follow the course of our principles. The glorious sparseness that is necessary and enduring, the analytics that belong to us, the terms that are worn out but necessary, crammed with an inexcusable desire: waiting for history to manifest itself. We go on coexisting linearly with a period that isn't right for us, ever skinnier as we are, and severe, maintaining an eloquent silence in the face of everything that is outside our convictions. Yes, because beyond the vacuous but foreseeable movements that govern us, is certainty, our certainty, embedded in the militant corner where what's perennial about our brains resides.

Your reforming ideas were checked and disseminated. You understood. You do understand, I said to you, that it's not possible for you, you of all people, to fall into the trap, what trap, what are you talking about, why are you interrupting me, let me think. The kettle's not boiling now, it's not boiling, stupid gas. Did you want, on that day, your most reformist day, to think, what were you going to think? You were on the verge of giving up the line and entering the complicated territory of negotiations. You were headed straight to dissipation, to abandonment and to the most enormous failure. You were looking for a way out as if you'd been transformed into a mole. Let me think, let me think.

I laughed.

Something outside had already disintegrated, I thought about disintegration, about its causes, about its effects, about the whole extensive monotony that would be surrounding us. Swiftly a succession of fragments was projected in my head, altered to the point of exploding: balances of power, working-time, use value, exchange value. I sensed the fortuitous and swift movement of a technological net sliding across a fake digital sign: 'The bourgeoisie has stripped of its halo every occupation hitherto honoured and looked up to with reverent awe. It has converted the physician, the lawyer, the priest, the poet, the man of science, into its paid wage labourers.'

An eager fragment that spread, projecting a work that was not only ultra-technological but undoubtedly of an unsuspected contemporaneity, a wild opera that showed its violence. The same violence that your migraine causes you now, the discomfort on its arbitrary and persistent course, the ominous sharp prick. I want to touch your head, to help you with the pain, walk it through your skull to dislodge it, pass through the brain, running over its folds, to take that pain out through your eye, expel it towards the walls of the room until it has been dissolved and destroyed. Lie down. Close your eyes, I'll get you a tea. Why don't you shut up, yeah you, you're the one who's causing me pain, you. And in rage you stutter over the words, but then when you were about to quit and take another path, your own, you fell silent, focused, immersed in the last body that then belonged to you and that was now in clear retreat. Self-absorbed from head to toe, caught in the tension, in yours. You were, I know it, about to decide. What could I offer you, you looked at me, I now think, with the surprise of an aggressive and uncertain resignation. You knew, of course you did, that we were in a dilemma. The cell was hanging by a thread, if you were a part of it, if you went back to gather up the pieces, you would go deeply into an irrevocable decision, you'd go right to the centre of the cell to persuade, you'd arrive, after the urgency of the call, at a clandestine and unpostponable meeting to seek an agreement, your agreement, yours in which a position would be decided upon, yes, a "position", you'd told me in the previous hours, changing position, we need to go in, you said, some other way, because the conditions of production have altered and that involves, you said, assuming a new position, you understand?

Yes, I understood.

They always change, I said, conditions of production always do, but not the position, no, only the conditions of production, which are masked and devious and crooked. How are you going to change position? If you change position, I said, we'll be on our way out, fleeing towards a readable common territory, to the new terrain of incendiary, ravenous ideology and then I quoted, verbatim: 'Modern industry has established the world market, for which the discovery of America paved the way.' Ah, you said, ah, disappointed or unresolved or looking for some way of agreeing with me. You wanted, or that was how I understood it, to find an ally in me, you wanted me to accompany you to a new meeting of the cell, you waited doubtful, worried, for me to join in. But I didn't.

The meeting room, the last one, the one in which your defeat would be consolidated, felt uncomfortable, and yet, at the same time, perfectly safe. There we were, how many of us?, eight or ten sitting on those chairs worn out by use, all clandestine (the eight are still sitting at the corner of this room, their faces or rather the outlines of their features experiencing the effects of a protracted mutism: the petrification of their mouths and some very ill-treated teeth). I can recall only the room from those final months because we needed to change spaces, avoid addresses, rethink neighbourhoods, blocks, corners, the composition of houses, moving about with rational wariness. We did it so as to avoid possible detection, the demolishing of our cell, we operated in those days according to the model of a beehive, the image of the bee. The walls, the ceiling were there to remind us just how provisional the space was. I looked carefully at the ceiling, went over the walls, paused on the expressions, focused on the shifting of the attendees' feet, their movements. I devoted myself to scrutinising. The final meeting had been unleashed. The decimated chairs, the restless feet, the faces that longed for neutrality, I've already said: the walls, the ceiling, the coffee, the inexcusable lack of sugar and its acidic dregs, the thermos, the plastic cups, the lukewarm sips. The wait. Your ally, and myself, the imminent conflict, the nuances of the arguments, the hostile tiredness that had lethally invaded our cell.

My attention was held by the attendees' legs. Their restless movements betrayed a nervousness, but I returned particularly to the horror of that night and to the chest collapsed by a breathing that was becoming accelerated and progressively impossible, we've got to take the boy to hospital, while the implacable death rattle placed my protest, my urgency, my desperation in the centre of nothing, because the words were there to cover up his death, to accompany it and perhaps to hasten it with words that were useless, words that were shrouds, elemental and primitive at the impotence of the asphyxia that was happening centimetres from faces which from that moment were going to empty out, our own, those faces we would carry and which would charge us with the incomprehensible act of surviving.

Later, when our faces began to be ratified by age, we reached an agreement not to remember. We decided to suspend all judgement of the past. Who made that decision, how was our pact formed, could it perhaps have been implicit, I wonder now. We submerged ourselves in the room, our room, the same one as in past years, how many years, twenty, thirty, forty, could it be a hundred or more, it hardly matters. Both of us punctual in the room, clinging stubbornly to the validity of our routines. I hold the cup of tea out to you, I don't complain about the cold I had to put up with in the kitchen, I add the sugar, stir the liquid with the spoon, bring the cup closer to you, you lean in, drink, you do it with pain imprinted on your face, brow, cheek and especially on your ferociously crushed jaw, the old injury, holding out and, of course, your eyes, the look in your eyes tired or worn out or fed up with the headache, the look, yes, your look, decisively altered by the migraine. Or not. A look that pretends I'm not here, that I do not stretch out my arm to provide you with the tea, that I have not been to the kitchen and then returned with my stealthy tread, my foam slippers, I observe them, their shape, the workings of that precise and worn and fragile and even childish foam on my feet, but I should say, our slippers, the only ones we have. My feet, which in some sense are unknown, feet captured on rigid, functional journeys, lightly covered by some really quite dreadful slippers, I look at them, I look at the slippers, as I sit on the edge of the bed and my pupil reaches the perimeter of the floorboards, at the exact moment when my eyes produce an inevitable blink, so quick, that mechanical quickness of the body's, the same quickness that allows me to get up, take the now empty cup and hold it relatively firmly, raise myself from my ridiculous slippers and look at you and blink once again and try, try to ask you why didn't we take him, why, I say, didn't we take him and I don't, as usual, finish the phrase. And you know I'm not going to complete the question, but you understand that I'm not going to forget it and we are going to be held suspended in it, in a key question that has no answer and that only works like this, as a question, not an idle one, no, never that, but rather the unequivocal way in which I protect myself in order to remember and to remind you how much we need to submit, to what point we are committed from the most unusual root of our bones.

Yours, mine, I think, while I keep looking at my feet and their compact arrangement of innumerable bones, do you want to, I say, read the paper.

I can't, you answer, not now.

We follow, at a distance, and even with an ostensible coldness, the events into which the always collapsed present organises itself. Each time we read the newspaper, we spare ourselves any comments, we deliberately do not demonstrate surprise and still less astonishment at the exaggeration of the headlines. We just exchange fleeting smiles when some excess verges on the pathetic. We smile and maybe even shake our heads to confirm the degree that the outrage has reached. We know to perfection the grotesque alienation of the headlines as well as the exercise of synthesis demanded by a professional reading, the acute probing that the news requires. After all we were analysts perhaps for too long. We learned to handle each of the variables, not just to weigh them up but to establish their intricate relationships. Analysts. We remained watchful, engrossed, deciphering. We acted, fulfilling our work as militants. The mistakes we made at the beginning of our roles we were able to correct thanks to our exhaustive passion. Analysts of headlines, of paragraphs, of cross sections, of simultaneities and differences, of nuances, of plots, the insatiable repetition of a piece of news, the coarse manipulation. In the manner of a jigsaw puzzle or a disjointed map, we re-established the territory. You don't want to read the paper, you can't because of your headache. No, you've told me, you repeat it with a scornful wave of your hand. Do you remember, I ask you, and I feel myself penetrated by a breath of life passing through me, but you interrupt my words.

No, you say, no, I don't remember.

I move down the aisle, steadying myself on each metal bar in turn. My body doesn't stop shaking. Not until the bus comes to a complete halt, and I step down carefully onto the pavement. Nobody but me has got out at this stop today. I have the number of streets I need to cross in my mind, five of them. Yes, five, I think, as I imprint a steady rhythm onto each of my steps. Quickly now. Today there's an icy morning wind harrying me. I'm going to have to put up with this premature cold to reach the house where they're expecting me.

Right outside number 509 I stop and press the doorbell. The maid lets me in. I greet her briefly and walk straight to the bedroom. The moment I'm inside, I shut the door behind me. I register the pleasant heating that protects the room. I partly draw the curtains, taking care not to let all the light escape. Straight away I undress: coat, dress, tights, shoes. I feel her watching me from the bed as, from inside my bag, I quickly pull out the plastic smock and put it on. Then I fold my clothes and place them on top of the only chair in the room, the one positioned right beside her bed. I rub my hands energetically and lean towards her:

Today we've got to have a bath, I say.

She watches me passively with her huge, watery eyes. When I run my hand over her face, I notice her rough skin and see that her mouth is edged with a lumpy white line. I look in the nightstand drawer and use the paper towel smeared with cream to clean the clots from her mouth. I do it with a movement that is swift but careful.

Up we get, I say. We're going to get up now.

Deep in her eyes a profound unease appears.

She shakes her head, no. But I climb onto the bed, put pressure on her shoulders to get her sitting up. I know how to make her sit up and also how to get her legs down. To do this, I support her back, I push her hips and, with one quick movement, I get off the bed myself and lift her up propelling her with her own arms. I do it gently because I know how much her joints hurt her.

When we are standing, she steadies herself against my shoulder with a strength that never ceases to surprise me. Before we take a first step, I am careful that her feet don't get tangled with the hem of her nightie.

Let's walk slowly. Nice and slow, I say.

She's angry and I can read a mixture of terror and contempt in her look. I turn my eyes away, I hide them. We reach the bathroom door, I open it and immediately move her close to the wall and put her hands on the metal bars so she can support herself. She stands there with her head tilted in anticipation. She waits for me to raise her arms and carefully take off her nightie. She's shivering. I run the shower and adjust the temperature till it's just right. I turn back towards her and rub her arms. At that moment, I bend down and remove her underwear and diaper. I take the wet underwear and leave it beside the nightie. I wrap the diaper in a piece of plastic and throw it in the rubbish bin.

The smell is an assault.

But I've already got her covered by the water and I take care for her head not to be exposed to the jet as it crashes down. I redirect the water and soak the sponge with soap, the same sponge I personally bought, the best, and slide it energetically between her legs. Although I don't look at her face, I know she's keeping her eyes closed. Always.

I squeeze and squeeze the sponge I've used to clean her crotch, until I've made sure that, down the drain, amid a circle of water, the last remains of shit that were still left around her genitals is slipping away. I run the sponge over her again, this time without soap, to tidy her up.

The smell begins to lose its consistency. All that remains is the heavy aura of urine that has definitively invaded the bedroom and the bathroom. As if it had taken shelter on the walls, that urine smell, constant, rebellious, unmistakeable.

Now we're going to turn around, I say. Best turn slowly, so we don't slip.

She likes this. My running the sponge over her back, slipping over it smoothly thanks to the fine quality of the soap I recommended myself. It's flaky, her back. I stoop down and keep my eye on the shape of her legs. I feel the water from the shower wetting my hair. I forgot to bring my plastic cap. I realised this when I opened my bag. I don't have the cap, I thought, knowing full well that it was already too late to mend the fault. When I finish on her legs, I straighten up and dry my hair with one of the white towels. There are two. I asked for that specifically. Two towels.

Let's turn around again, I say.

I support her shoulders and position her in front of me. Our eyes meet and I make a point of unloading my gaze, of looking at her as if we did not exist.

Let's close our eyes, I say.

She closes them and tilts her head. I've already got the shampoo in the palm of one hand, ready to begin a difficult stage. I keep her head away from the stream and start washing her hair.

Don't you open your eyes now, I say. Don't open them because this could sting. Keep those eyes closed nice and tight, I say again.

With my fingertips I rub her skull until her hair is soft and disappears under the copious foam. She still has hair, I think, she must have had a lot of it, too much, I think, while I see the water start to drip off and I remove the foam that's about to slide down from her forehead. I position her head beneath the shower and soak her hair. From her tilted head, the foam overflows directly onto her chest and at that moment I start to sponge her down and cover the accumulation of dark, irregular marks scoring her stomach.

With the sponge I move what little is left of her breasts and I see her wrinkled, darkened nipples, with the edge of a nail I detach the little black flakes I had noticed previously. She still has her eyes closed, squeezed shut, so tightly that her face is distorted by a grimace.

Let's get those little eyes open now, I say.

I bend down with the sponge on the front of her legs and again the water soaks my head. I end at her ankles, get up and take the towel to dry my hair again. Then I turn off the tap and wrap her in the towel. I look in the dresser for the drier and, thanks to the heat, her hair resumes its shape. Then I dry my own.

I take hold of her shoulders, walk her wrapped in the white towel slowly towards the bedroom.

Let's sit down, I say.

I sit her on the edge of the bed and make sure the towel is covering her. Then I go to the cupboard and find, in the assigned drawer, a clean nightie. The sky-blue cotton is discoloured and the flowers adorning it are almost impossible to make out. I look in the top part of the cupboard for a diaper. The huge bags are squeezed in there, in a space that seems inadequate. I take out a diaper and arrange it on her.

I remove the towel and lay her on her back. Her legs hang off the edge of the bed. With the blanket that's on top of the bedspread, I cover her down to her waist. I open the nightstand drawer, I take out the cream and the oil and put the oil down on the surface.

Let's get those legs open now, I say.

She doesn't want to open them, so I am forced to do it, to open her legs myself. I smear my right hand with cream, and I apply the restorative cream, vertically, all the way down her crotch. Between what sparse hairs she still has, I can see that a large expanse of irritated skin has begun to spread and grow.

You've been scratching, I say. We don't need to scratch ourselves.

The critical state of her skin tells me that a wound is about to be unleashed that I think looks dangerous. The skin looks ready to break and for that reason I take care to cover that area especially with a considerable and perhaps excessive amount of cream. It will pass, in any case, I think, this wound. It hurts her. I know because she complains faintly. If I looked up I'd be able to see the grimace of pain on her face. But I don't because I notice she's getting cold and I still need to apply the oil. I leave the tub of cream on the top of the nightstand and pick up the oil.

I kneel down and move on to her feet. I separate each of her toes in turn and cover them in oil. I ought to cut her nails, but I postpone it. Not now, I think. Then I lie her on the bed, I put her face-down and cover her with the blanket from hip to feet. I notice that the skin on her back is goose-pimpled.

Are you cold?, I ask.

I spread the oil over her neck and then move milli-metre by millimetre down her back. Her skin is so dry, I don't worry about how much oil I'm getting through. Then I pull the blanket over her back and proceed to lubricate her thighs. I notice the vulnerability of the skin on her hip. Very soon the bedsores will be triggered, I think. I turn her around and cover her down to the waist while the oil now moves over her pelvis and upper legs.

I take the diaper and I yank her up by the waist and fit it onto her. I make sure it is perfectly arranged, tightening the tabs, over and over so it doesn't come undone. I immediately put on her underwear, then I lower the blanket and set about oiling her breasts and stomach. I go quickly with the oil and I know we're approaching the moment that's trickiest between us. Her face. The oil on her face.

I have no choice.

I put the oil onto my hand and my fingers begin to feel around her face. She openly tries to dodge me, twisting her head. As ever, stubborn, wilful. Her.

Let's keep our head nice and still now, I say.

Her movement obliges me to take her jaw in my left hand to keep her still while I cover her cheeks with the oil. She opens her eyes and looks at me with a spitefulness that is piercing.

Faggot, she says.

Now let's get our nightie on, shall we? Sit up now, I say.

I straighten her up, and put on her nightie. I open the nightstand and take out the small brush. As I comb her hair, I am careful to disentangle the strands gently, then I lie her back down, arrange the sheets, smooth the bedcover and position the pillows beneath her head. She looks healthy, somehow renewed, now that there's a little colour in her cheeks.

You're looking well, I say to her. You're looking very well, I insist.

I put away the cream, the oil and the brush in the nightstand drawer. I pick up my clothes: my shoes, the handbag, the towel, and go to the bathroom. I get dressed and run the hairdryer over every crease of the smock.

When the plastic is dry, I fold it and put it into my handbag. I tidy away the hairdryer and leave the nightie, the panties and the two wet towels in the laundry basket. I confirm that everything is in its place. I check the taps, straighten the lid of the rubbish bin that contains the dirty diaper, switch off the light and shut the door.

I walk over to the bed and a simple glance confirms a kind of serenity and order. This time she hasn't moved, nor thrown the pillows on the floor, nor messed up the sheets. I open the curtains and walk across the room.

See you soon, I say.

I go out into the hallway and am assailed by the silence encircling the house.

I'm done, I call out, not quite shouting. I pause in the hallway till the servant appears with the envelope in her hand. I take it, and put it away in my handbag. We walk over to the front door together. Standing in the doorway, she says:

It's cold.

Yes, I say, it's cold.

You'll come next Tuesday?, she asks.

Yes, I answer. Yes, of course.

We think obsessively about eyes, mine, yours, our eyes. We look over the human atlas, the most compact kind, but in reality our attention is focused on the disintegration of its parts, the excessive and cunning amplification of each organ and there, of course, that enormous eye with its intricate relationships. It's frightening, that eye, monstrous and multi-branched. How can we bear it, how could we live with eyes that would get worn out until progressively they began to attack the purpose and the direction of the gaze. I look at your eye. I open your eye as wide as I can with my fingers.

Let me look at your eye.

What for?, you say. To see it, to check the eye. Fine, fine, you answer and allow my fingers to go to considerable trouble, to open it, mocking your eyelid, to thus reveal your hideous eyeball to the point that it seems outside itself. I've got your eye open between my fingers. A living, moving, solid eye, but it is perishing, I know, this eye. I bring the small lamp closer and closer, but it's not enough for my own eye, this familiar ocular frailty. If I had a flashlight, a microscope, the power of a lamp that was more than halogen. The eyelid contracts, I tell you, every six seconds. Every six seconds there's a blink. I try to get inside, try to understand the eye that is dragging us down.

Every six seconds?, you say.

Exactly.

You laugh, in your way, self-contained, rational, lacking in realism. I experience this incredible desire to say:

Don't laugh, or to say: what are you laughing at, or to say: why are you laughing.

The eye doesn't see anything, I say, it doesn't, not ever, it's the brain, I say, it's a command, that's what it is. I try to put a special slant on it, that word, command, to emphasise it and, as always happens to me, to my regret, I repeat the word and add: it delivers a command to the optic nerve. I'm sure that's how it is and yet allow myself to be invaded by the doubt that assails me when faced with the reality of the collusion between the brain and the optic nerve. I explore with one of my fingertips, from my left hand, your eyeball.

I touch it.

It's watery.

A liquid that's cold and thin, crystalline. I mean this: crystalline. You shake your head, you can't, you want to blink, you'd like me to remove my fingers that are holding an absurd eyelid and thus retrieve your eye. I'd like to say, who cares about your eye, who cares about the six seconds your eyelids can bear. Instead, robotically, I refer to the vitreous humour and to the aqueous humour. This is why I have the possibility of running one of my fingertips gently over your eyeball and being sure that this brushing does not hurt you because what I am really touching is the aqueous humour that's there for protection. That is what I do. But it's no use. I cannot understand the nature of your eye or of mine and its looking is something I can only presume. In its greatest fullness or in its decline there's the look, aqueous and vitreous, but cerebral, a cerebral look, yours or ours, a look that is fundamentally nervous but entirely dominated by a brain that we are used to managing. A look, this is what we decided, that is opportune, external. A look that is attentive and consolidated into history. We cannot, you said to me, lapse into the sentimentality that the most predictable side of our age has in store for us.

Yes, I answered, I agree.

We should, this is what you said, be careful about the deviationisms that are watching us. Yes, I answered, they're watching us everywhere. For that reason, I said, you must remember that: 'All property relations in the past have continually been subject to historical change consequent upon the change in historical conditions.'

While I was writing those words, I thought about how I must not get them wrong. A single poorly written syllable or a spelling mistake would tarnish the statement's prestige. Then, it would itself be entering the territory of deviationism, an exceptional syllogism would intervene perversely which was there to persuade. It was a matter of understanding and then copying. It was a strategic task. I had been chosen to fulfil the mission the cell had entrusted to me. The first cell, that one we set up and which had not yet experienced division, the first of each of the successive atomisations that the years would precipitate.

A studious copyist, the person charged with selecting the imperative teachings. I had been delegated to channel the discomfort wisely. You insisted: we've got to clear out any sentimentality because otherwise our cell will be transformed into a stronghold that's too volatile. I endorsed, I did, your perspective. I no longer remember how I was chosen to be delegated, how the voting was carried out, if I volunteered or was simply pushed into fulfilling this task. Do you remember, I ask you, how I came to be the one delegated? With your hands, you take my fingers off your eyelid. You close your eye, both your eyes. You squeeze them.

Yes, you say, I remember.

Well then, I say, how was it? Ah, ah, you answer, visibly bothered. I get up off the edge of the bed where I had been keeping your eye beneath my gaze and walk over towards the table. I sit on the chair and study the eye mentally. I extract it from its context and go over each of its parts. Quickly. In this way I put what brain I still have to the test and I understand the eye better. I know I copied the words, the syllables precisely and I managed to do full justice to my own role. I know that afterwards, when the months were already going by, I vaguely made a mistake. I was wandering, thinking about how to attain a new status. I wanted to participate from a place that was less opaque or submissive. What I was looking for was to occupy a space, that space I had designed myself.

It was a legitimate wish. Rising up to the surface of the cell. This led me into a mistake, the only barely perceptible lapse I committed. I did it because I was going back over the organogram to secure myself a new role in which I would be able to feel. It was just that I didn't feel any more while one by one I copied the words that I myself had chosen. Suddenly they started to lose their purpose or simply distanced themselves from my hand. I left out a word, which subverted the sentence. That word broke the order of time, the verb that governed the letters' most intense trajectory. It just happened. Then it was too late. My copy, careless and imperfect, spun wildly around, changing the syllogism's meaning.

I was ashamed. Doubly so.

My silence transformed into shame and the fact that nobody recognised my mistake made it worse. This impunity let me understand that I was an expert now and I had no competition. But all the same, despite the primitive arrogance that assailed me, I didn't want to continue in my duty as copyist.

I did not renounce the function that had been asked of me, let alone the time I dedicated to choosing those statements that might enlighten. I had been elected precisely for what was recognised as an aptitude. Today

I can believe that that was what we shared, certain aptitudes that allowed us to come together. Except on the day when tedium must have assailed me and I abruptly broke the regulations. The cell, the first one, that one where we'd assigned roles, our cell, so small, small, but dedicated, its parts perfectly in gear, a harmonic cell governed by our most youthful years and which gave us confidence in ourselves and in our huge capacity for discretion, just at those moments when we could have been more talkative and could have become detached, but no, we didn't do it for love of our mother cell, but I, that day, eaten away by a discomfort I was unable to locate, asked in a haughty tone, which I can recognise as unacceptable today, about the need to commit to the grassroots.

Yes, that day, the day when an inexpressible sensation possessed me, you were working impeccably as secretary and I checked that everything was in order, that each person managed to supply a rigorous account of their activities. None of us could have questioned the effectiveness of your leadership, but it wasn't your leadership that prompted in me a sensation close to distress, it was the narrow total of bodies repeated so monotonously over the course of more than a year. The same ones, weekly, punctilious, serious, responding. I was one of the ones who made up the monotonous series, a component that no longer caused any surprise.

Ten?, were there ten of us?, I ask you, from the chair.

Yes, you answer me, distracted. I don't trust your answer. I look at the curled-up ball into which you have contained yourself and see the way you ruin your bones with the terrible position that shelters you in the bed. Your legs, your shoulders, the spine, the tight frown, the twisted arms, the fingers. How will you survive, I ask myself, how are you going to survive curled up in the bed. What will become of your bones, I ask myself, what will their fate be if they even still have one, I say, some surviving trace of fate. At what level will the most acute, constant of pains break out, through the outline of your curled-up body. Where exactly will the pain be located, in what way will it shift about and how will you be able to move your knee or your elbow, in what space of your body will you still have an area free that doesn't torture you with its implacable stabbing already inscribed in the faulty marrow of your bones. What will your hours be like, I ask myself, as you melt and melt into the ball into which you are transforming before my eyes, these watery eyes, captured by an optic nerve that is operated like a puppet by the brain, my brain, just to watch your form in the bed, our bed, and sense the advancing of the solid bone pain you inflict on yourself and which belongs to you. Your bones, they're yours, I think, yours, but I have no conviction, projected as I am like a duplicate beside you, yes, both curled up into a ball on the bed. But now I see you from my chair and I also see how I suddenly burst in.

The grassroots, I said, where are the grassroots, what's the work that's done with the grassroots. After a moment of silence, a silence that was dramatic, contrived, theatrical, I went on: it's necessary (I had to correct myself), it's becoming necessary for us, for the correct course of our cell, to commit to the grassroots because: 'The ideas of the ruling class are in every epoch the ruling ideas.' It was a coup de théâtre. To achieve it, I used one of the last bits of copying I'd thrown myself into, maybe not the most exact one, but it was the one that came completely into my head at that moment. Along with the tone of voice, I was careful to maintain a facial expression supplied with a moderate degree of neutrality, I controlled those movements of my feet that might give me away, I tried to keep my hands in a state of calm. I even worried about where

I was aiming my gaze, no one in particular, no one the target of my eyes. A look that was general, but also blind. A look without a look.

A hollow remained, discomfort took hold. The other eight members of the cell were overtaken by fear and disbelief at a dissenting voice. There was briefly a cellular crisis, the cell itself went into a state of tension because my words, motivated by contradictory reasons that I myself could not adequately grasp, burst cruelly out to poison our matter and perhaps undo it altogether.

I might say now that there was an organic reason propelling me forward. I was carrying a biological discomfort within my body that urged me to provoke the first crisis. I don't remember my pain, I don't know which organ, which point in the body. Later, when the meeting had ended, I fell into a state of stupor. But you, the secretary, the best equipped of us, did not express even a flicker of displeasure, you answered serenely and managed, in a sense, to restore equilibrium. Years later, when the unknowns between us had all been toppled, I understood that I'd acted as a part of you, that it was you who had pushed me in some mysterious way to create the disturbance, the disturbance you so needed to validate your precision. I didn't seek to exonerate myself when I realised it because I needed these performances, mine, yours, these always perfect performances that we had to repeat in each of the cells we made up.

How did we do it? I look at you. I see you diffusely because the light or the strength of my eyes, I'm not sure, is starting to fade now. I'd like to get over to the bed and lie down and look out at the street. But no window exists and to us the street is a hieroglyph.

Always.

Surrendered to the discipline that a militant requires, we fulfilled our orders to the letter. We walked, following our own steps. The whole time we needed to walk behind one another, looking at our own backs. Thus we were transformed into our own guards. Thus you began to tire, thus you became less visible, thus you came apart, thus you disappeared. And thus I see you right now surrendered to exploring your own insides. Do you have it, I wonder, do you still have a speck of interiority. What are you thinking about?, I ask you, but before you answer me I know in advance what you're going to say: nothing. Nothing, you say, and this time I believe you. You're thinking about nothing. We're thinking the same. About nothing. Always.

Already, in a sense, five decades have passed (no, no, a thousand years). Five decades that have slipped by giving no more than a super-precarious account of that time, of mine, of our time. Trapped in the last five decades that had to contain us. I could, I know, sound out the decades, ten by ten, break down the years and their focus, identify a drawn-out place for each occurrence, come to consolidate a version that is possible and, even more than that, truthful. But aren't we, I say to myself and then I can't go on because I realise the question I'm asking is useless. That's just how it is, since inside, within the wretchedness of each of the decades or in their fleeting luxuries and even when they're at their most shapeless we take root so, so very sparsely that we prove inscrutable. In truth we have dodged the reality of each of the decades, we were only able to participate on their perimeter like tiny rodents in constant flight. However, however, I said to you emphasising the repetition, that's how history is constructed. I felt, as I said it, the weight of an unforgivable grandiloquence and it was all I could do to avoid it, to repent for having used such a convenient or such a hollow expression. I was talking to myself, of course, alone in the room because you were pretending to be asleep or playing the sick man while you breathed in the bed avoiding as far as possible giving away the fact that you were inhaling, that you were exhaling, thus concealing the existence of your body in the bed, in our bed, of my body in the bed. Perhaps the most sensible thing would be to say once and for all: our body, to accept that we're merged into one single cell, into the cell we are and which is now propelling us towards the crisis, a cellular crisis or a deteriorated cellular condition, yes, transformed into a true republic of cells that confirms us as organic, too organic or congenital, don't touch me, don't touch me with your foot, I say to you, my ankle, don't do it, move your foot, get it out of the bed. Take your foot off if you need to, cut it off, die.

He's dying, he's dying, I thought. We thought it together, said it together, he is dying. I saw or we saw, I no longer know how to be fair, the fragility of the human machine or else we observed the human as a contempt-ible organisation, common and mechanical, a primi-tive and unceasing form, generating the worst type of exploitation, a merely organic production that was there only to serve its own species, the human species. Yes, a serial, mass-produced machinery that existed to colonise itself, the human species, I say, we say, in a process that isn't even complex but exploitative in what it was hiding. What was it hiding?, that which is elided, the fact that the body, the countless organisms were there to serve other organisms as a production line that carried a compo-nent that was dehumanising, inexcusable and unfair. The division of bodies, the wearing away of organs, who said that?, who? But death was coming to us and it was then, I think or we think, I don't know any more, that a lucid, alarming moment was unleashed that allowed us to understand that we were pieces of machinery. What happened might be seen as an epiphany or a moment of understanding, on the bed, while we thought about how to do it, how to take him to the hospital, how to get him into the hospital and to secure for the boy, my own, my boy, a bed that was technical, decent and effective and get hold of oxygen and medication and a drip and a doctor, a medical team who would, at least, try. I thought this or we thought it, how to save him, how to avoid him dying on the bed, our bed, the only one we had, the one we have still, this bed that consummated death and that condemns us to a waiting that reasserts itself as waiting and that seems capable only of accumulating decades (millennia) of erosion and ruin, of dead cells, of decay in pillows or in the totally faded sheets, even more than the thin blanket that is progressively losing its source of warmth, its shape, its weight, its geometric limits, an insubstantial rectangle that was once luminous and exact. I watched the death machine exterminating the cell machine. From then on we became mere cells, that was all.

Move your foot over, I say, and you do it.

In this way I free up a small space for my leg, I struggle with you to establish jurisdiction over the tiny territory we possess, a dispute over the place where feet, our feet, get into position, determined not to get mixed up. That is why I say to you: move your foot over, to separate yours from mine. I even pretend the foot is mine and your bones belong to you, that my hip is not yours nor the pain in my kidneys. Move your foot over, I insist, despite knowing you've done it, I do it to save my leg from a terrible and implacable confusion. I want to believe that your leg belongs to you, that it's yours, from the revulsion its contact provokes in me, the brushing with your foot covered in its sock, because never skin between us, not ever that, but all the same I need to understand that the foot covered in a sock that cannot be borne is not mine, terrified at the possibility of sharing a common leg, the risk, the doubt that forced me to ask you if it was my leg or yours, because it was bothering me, it was bothering me, it's yours, you said to me, that leg. Mine?, I said, mine?, struck through with astonishment and I linked my fingers through my fingers to check, but I wasn't sure even then because of that vague, incessant revulsion, because of that liquid and acidic burning that ran through me, that runs through me right now and while you move your foot, I feel mine fleeing from my body to rush over to your side, the side you occupy in the bed.

I ought to think about our foot and the bed would be more possible, it would be more agreeable and it would put an end to a disturbance that has become unsustainable. Our foot. But the disgust resurfaces, a physical sensation that cannot be avoided, the disgust at your foot that takes in your hip and the face you possess and that is unmanageable to me. I turn around, disciplined, towards the wall and I wait.

We are, so we agreed, a cell.

We did it after the death had to be consummated, don't move, not your head let alone your arms, not now, because it was a death that was up to us and that tore us apart. We didn't take him to the hospital, it didn't seem like a possibility. My entreaties, I know, were nothing but rhetoric, a kind of excuse or evasion. We could not go with his body so diminished and dying, panting and dying, gaunt and dying, beloved and dying, to the hospital, because if we did, if we transported his dying agony there, if we moved it from the bed, we would put the entirety of the cells at risk because our own cell would fall and its destructive wake would start exterminating the whole threatened, diminished militant field. Although we had our instructions, we didn't know what to do with his death, where we would take his death, how we would legalise it, nor did we know how to come out of civil non-existence to enter with his body into a grave in a funeral procession that might give us away.

There is no mystery at all between night and the body, between tiredness and night, between uncontrollable sleep and night. I know I will sleep anyway, I know

we will get through the insomnia and, in the unmanageable empty wasteland of our sleeping bodies, we will be
able to give way to these limbs of ours, I understand that
we will brush against each other inconveniently, I understand and, even more than this, I keep on the lookout
for your foot crushing mine or your arm on my hip
or the contact of our shoulders or our heads, too close,
breathing in monotonous synchrony. Yes, we breathe
next to each other or one behind the other or back
to back with each other. We breathe. We do that. He's
hardly breathing, not breathing at all and I remember
how we cried together, the tears fell with no modesty
or no control and especially no trace at all of shame, we
cried as I repeated, we've got to take him to the hospital
and you, as you cried, you shook your head, saying no
and you were trying, seeking, with your hand, with what
you had at that time, when your hand was still real and
belonged to you, to touch his face, to run your hand
down his face with a gentleness, a firmness and a distress
I didn't recognise in you. You touched his face, ran over
it again, wanting to preserve it in the lines of your hand,
but your tears confirmed that, no, it wasn't possible, that
you were finally going to lose your hand when his face
ended, the memory of your own hand. A face that was
on its way out and which I now struggle to reconstruct.
Do you remember, I say to you, what his face was like,
I say it with my own turned towards the wall and I feel
you moving, you battling, not wanting to. And because
you don't want to, that's why you bury your elbow in my
ribs knowing full well I cannot stand your elbow in my
ribs let alone your trying to be conciliatory, by means
of your hand on my head, the fright. That was what you
tried, putting your hand on my head the first time I asked
if you were still holding his face and I experienced the
fierce explosion of a retching, the bile that was eating

away at me, a retching that came undeniable and resonant and aggressive, a biliary response that was finding its
way from the complaint of a too mortified liver that was
making its presence felt to say no, no to a hand on the
head, on mine, your hand. I said no, no, no, please, as the
bile fell onto the bed leaving the blanket ravaged, even
more, and then you went out that night, that sole night on
which you dared to go out, with your possible sorrowful
steps along an unwelcoming pavement, the dangerous
cement of the open air in which you sheltered yourself
or sought yourself, you exposed yourself in order to flee
from the retching, from the bile, from the overwhelming
cloud of a face we were already forgetting.

Both of us.

But what we would never be able to forget was his
immanence and hence the bile and the failure of your
going out and your return heavy with bitterness and
with silence.

I notice how you get up from the bed now, you put
on my slippers and leave the room. But you don't go to
the bathroom, you don't do it and my amazement grows
when I realise you're headed for the kitchen, that after
operating the light-switch, after obtaining the austere or
stingy glow of the 25-watt bulb, you light the fire on the
stove, take the aluminium kettle and put it on the flame
and while you wait, numb, for the boiling, you press
your temples with your fingers. I know that even though
you're standing up you keep your shoulders amazingly
hunched and as you sway, you're thinking about the
lime-scale on the bottom of the kettle, the alarming
amount of built-up lime-scale, but you quit this contaminating image, you cast aside the glimmer of concern
and resume your habitual indifference. You return to the
room with your cup of tea and place it on the safest part
of the nightstand. You do it in total darkness, guided by

the wisdom that time bestows upon the knowledge of spaces. You're on your side, on the bed, leaning on one of your elbows and sipping. Don't sip, I say to you, don't, why did you get up, what's got into you having tea at this time and moving around and waking me and forcing your sounds on me, what's up with you, what are you thinking, as if you were the only person, yes, the only person in this room, shut up, what do you mean shut up if you're the one who woke me up and between the words there appears the image of the tea.

Mildly, with the calm that can radiate from certain landscapes or the careful design of a room intended for rest, I think about the tea and about your premature attachment to that liquid. It was a custom you had, a curious detail, an anecdote that characterised you. Yes. Alongside your name there arose as if in a small caption your fondness for tea. Not wine, not beer, not even pisco. But tea was not able to diminish you or mock you, it was simply registered as a habit that was if not respectable, at least possible, a custom that everybody accepted and which never got in the way. I paused, I remember, on the tea.

That unexpected moment, when in the meeting, the one where you were named secretary, by means of a vote that was too naïve yet seemed so solemn to us, you managed to get a place, a space, a recognition that came to you days earlier or after having turned sixteen. We served together in the cell, that first, extraordinarily studenty one we had joined. After we had endured some chaotic meetings they asked or we asked if we might equip ourselves with some better form of organisation, an organisation that was, as they put it, organic. You became that cell's first secretary. When the results were confirmed, I couldn't resist a provocative impulse and I said to you: bureaucrat. You smiled, and yet after we said goodbye I didn't hear from you again until the following week, the week when you were already acting as secretary and you were dealing with the minutes and contributing active proposals for revitalising our cell.

I remember the cup of tea and your eyes seeking me out in the meeting. There, in public, among us handful of assembled adolescents, you reproached me for having forgotten one of the documents. I apologised serenely and even with some poise, I acknowledged my inexperience with the document and promised to make amends. Thus was conceived the thread in which we were going to be woven, your meticulous and outstanding secretaryship, an unstable place that I was to defend. This extended the thread of a fabric that today has merged us into a common strand that now seems impossible to disentangle. Mine, I say to you, the leg, it's mine, the knee, its bone and the ankle that ends at the beginning of the foot, the feeling of having a leg each time a movement occurred, the certainty of lying with a leg in bed.

No, you say to me, that one's mine and you say it with a voice that is verging on entreaty, leave my body alone, I'm so tired, let me have some peace, at least let me keep this leg of mine that still belongs to me.

You are curled up as usual, occupying the piece of the bed that my body is pursuing. But you can't, I can't, you say to me, and I hear you, believe you, understand you. I leave the bed to you on your own, I surrender it to you. Today you're so, so very curled up. I don't know how you can manage to stay so still, perfectly still, just leave me alone. And you don't close your eyes at all and the light enters you through one eye. I'm relieved at the light in your eye, it gives me a feeling of solid security that allows you your eye and the light and the little opening, so small, so small, between your eyelash that barely moves, yes, though it does flicker very slightly as the light reveals it, I mean, the thin thread of your eyelash and a little bit of eye. We're going to die, you say or almost say: we're dead or they killed us, you say. I no longer know what to believe from you and I look at you as if it's the first time I've ever seen an eye, subtly half-open, absurd, an eye nestled in the bed I so desire, I desire that bed with such fury, right this very moment. But you deserve it more than me, yes, you deserve to put your eye in the bed and stay there surrendered to the imperceptible movement of your eyelash on this century day that seems prepared to share out only the smallest portion of light.

You move, I leave you, I move away from the bed. I flee from what's left to you of your body. Let me sleep. You can't sleep, you say, but you sleep and sleep as if the world had already ended and you aren't going to keep your word to it. I understand you, I understand you. Something exists that is sticky though not irritating which is coming out of me just like the saliva that with parsimonious slowness drips from your lip onto the sheet. A tiny little thread. The sheet is not. It hasn't been for too long. You no longer complain. Never. I don't need to see how your thread of saliva descends a specific line that your cheek provides it with, I mean your lip and cheek. The lip indicates its inside that's wet, watered, but yes, cautious and dignified too. And in one decisive moment the cheek seems a single line that is joined by the eyelash and the half-open eye from the saliva that the light disturbs.

Or does not disturb. I understand how much they need each other, the eye and the light, the darkness and the light. The light tires. Holding back your saliva tires you too and you let it fall, roll, as if you didn't need it and wanted to remain liquid, watery, generous to the unrepentant sheet. You no longer complain. Never. Not about the sheet nor about the bed. You just want to be between them for a space of time that you cannot determine. You lie down fully clothed. Under the blanket I can make out your trousers. Always the same. You don't complain. Never. Never about the sharp little hole in the trousers that rubs roughly against your ankle till it prompts a subtle, tangential rash. Because although you move carefully and slowly, the trousers and their sharp little hole are exactly in a vulnerable area of the ankle. Everything seems to repeat itself. Ambiguous. Your shirt. I ask you, you know, to clean its cuffs and its collar, because it shows, it shows. With one of the edges of the shirt you touch your mouth each time you try to get out of bed. Always the same: you take out your hand, raise it and bring a corner of the shirt slowly to your mouth, dab the corners of your mouth twice and then, with the same cuff, always the right, you dry the damp part of your cheek. And only then do you arrange yourself on your elbow. You steady all the weight of your body on your elbow, you draw back the blanket and lower your legs until you're sitting on the edge of the bed. You bend down, you fold up the hem of your trousers to look at your leg and feel the very slightly reddened ankle. Then you look at me. Lie down, I say. You agree, you nod meekly and I could swear you were smiling. No, I couldn't swear it, though it does look like you're smiling. You stretch out one of your arms and allow the weight of your body to fall onto it. And you gradually loosen your arm and then you curl up again, you curl up in that position you seem to know so well, the one that brings you such relief. On your side, with one eye hidden and the other ready to look at me while you cover yourself back up with the blanket. But before letting your gaze lapse into a blind spot, you see me, only me so that I understand the value that is incarnate in that sort of smile. I know I can access only half of your smile because of the position in which you're lying in the bed.

You never lie on your back.

Never. Well yes, in reality you do lie on your back. You do it only after a while, only a few times. Then, as a result, although I can make out half of your mouth, half your smile, I answer you. Stay in bed, I say again. And at once I see how, with an express difficulty, you expand and occupy more and more space, an unprecedented amount of space, until practically the whole bed has disappeared beneath your body. You're like, I don't know, a dog. Meek, worn out, austere, wretched. You're like a dog. I move closer. I touch your brow, I put the palm of my hand on your brow and you shake your head. My hand bothers you, I can tell. I don't know why I did it, why I put my palm on your forehead, leave me alone.

Why did I have to put my hand on your forehead?

Just at the most unfortunate moment, when you had surrendered yourself to one of your periods of acute lethargy with yourself, at the moment when you had managed to stretch out your legs and turn over to face the ceiling of the room. You don't like looking at the ceiling. You try to avoid it. You prefer the wall. I know. The wall, I think, marks a boundary. I like it a lot too, the wall much more than the ceiling, I love the wall and its many irregularities. Seeing them one by one, discovering them one by one, being surprised by them, running a finger over the peeling paint, peeling it even more. Doesn't matter. I had to tell you, I told you with my back turned as one of my fingertips slid across the wall. I felt you behind me, pressing to get more space in the bed. Then I murmured: you're like a dog.

It sickened me, it pleased me, it was hard for me to say it.

Amidst a decisive silence, I stayed, I remained looking at the wall, playing with my finger in the paintwork and my knees bent so you could put yours right behind my legs and we'd fit together like two articulated stick figures or like two hinges condemned to agree on one wretched surface. The words dissolved and merged into the bed, they got tangled up in the blanket before disappearing camouflaged into the edges. Those edges that are already openly frayed. But you don't complain. Never. Nor do you tell me that the noise of my finger on the wall bothers you. The noise of the nail digging into the paint to test its fragile resistance.

I quickly pull my hand back from your forehead and understand that I should not look at you, that I need to be as though I wasn't there because you need some breathing space: for the room, the wall, the bed to be flooded with your breathing, with the emissions from your body, without me. I understand it, I get your need to amplify yourself in the room, yes, it's human, that you should seek to close or open your eyes, move a foot or not move it, open your often clenched hand or that you should be able to scratch without your elbow burrowing into my ribs and you stop, annoyed, openly intimidated by the brushing together of our bones.

Don't bother me, you murmur almost unintelligibly. I know I bother you just by being here. I don't need to put my hand on your forehead for your eyebrows to come together expressing the impatience that's passing across your frown. But I know, identically convinced, what you feel and how you feel when I go out and you take possession of the room. I know your relief. You inhale deeply enjoying the ritual of your own studied breath. I know you sit on the edge of the bed, stretch your spine and with both hands you hold the back of your waist to ease your kidneys, they're hurting you. I know you slide your feet slowly into my slippers and, still sitting on the bed, you look at how much your feet exceed my slippers and only then, after a long focused look, do you get up. I know that you walk, taking short, tired steps, around the room with the sole crucial purpose of loosening up your legs. I know you pause, you knead them and press on your calves. Then, you approach the bag, you open it, and sit on the bed to eat your bread. It's the thing you like most, bread, and you swallow it with an anarchic haste that might even be moving. You're hungry. And you go out into the hall to look for the bathroom, you walk, in a way, teetering, with your heels outside the slippers. In your hand you are carrying a piece of the newspaper and you scan it superficially and then you wipe your backside with it. You get a certain bearable revulsion from shit, its smell, yours. Always. The paper bothers you, everything irritates your skin. And you go back to the room and you try, you try, while an extreme and harmful moment is unleashed in you, to walk across the top of the floor-boards, but not only do you get worn out but your heels and thighs hurt, but specially you are driven crazy by the creaking coming from the floor's harsh irregularity, I know. And then, you climb up and submerge yourself in the bed, isolated, waiting for me to come back. You stay, you lie in the bed waiting for me. Incomprehensibly you count the time that's left to my arrival. You think blank, blank, blank until you hear my steps. You recognise them, I know you pick them out from some consider-able distance, that you measure how I'm approaching and approaching towards the room long before I open the door. Yes, my footsteps.

You're already lying down, I say as I come into the room.

You're already lying down. You blink, impassive. You don't answer. I walk over towards the wall and touch the bag hanging from the nail. With my hand on the cloth, I say, you ate your bread, you ate all the bread. I don't look at you while I take the bag down off the nail and one by one put in the bread rolls I've just bought and then, without ceremony, I launch myself at the bed and wipe off the crumbs that have been left on it. I lift up the blanket energetically and inevitably I completely shake you. You don't object. Instead you shut your eyes to avoid the sight of my hands and of my canines clattering with rage because you've eaten all the bread there was in the bag. Alert at the distance that allows you the sole act of shutting your eyes, you seek to dispel the hatred lodged in my canines by the quantity of crumbs scattered on top of the bed.

Then I go out into the hallway and walk down to the kitchen. I have the kettle in my hand, I turn on the tap and fill it with water. I light the blue flame, yes, right. I pause briefly at that contradictory blue until I get over its effect and cover it with the kettle. While I wait for it to boil, I allow my weight to fall completely onto one of my legs, then I let it fall onto the other. The water boils in time. I return to the room and on the usual tray, the only one, I put the two cups with the tea bags and what's left of the sugar.

Sit up.

You sit up and I hold the tea out to you, I add a little spoon of sugar. You stir the tea with the sugar. Sitting on the edge of the bed, I put the tray down on the floor and take hold of my cup. I notice how much the noise of my spoon bothers you. It disturbs you when I do it. You move towards the wall to leave me more space, but really you do it to escape from the sound of the metal. I try not to slurp, but it's inevitable some sound will get out. You slurp too. Well?, I say, well? Instead of answering, you return the cup to me with an undeniable sign of displeasure. And you sit there with your head leaning against the wall. I notice the outline that your head takes on, and I get a good look at your face. It happens to me sometimes: looking at you as if I'd never seen you before. And I find it surprising because your face loses its monotony and reappears before me with unexpected force. A face that is without antecedents. I look at you and I know that you notice my amazement.

It terrifies me that a face exists in you that's yours. Your nose scares me, and your mouth, and the imperturbable crack that your jaw has retained. I'm struck by the sight of that face, yours, against the wall. I register that it is your jaw, your nose and the inalienable outline of your face that is cut out against the peeling paint. The feeling that emerges in my mind is one of a joke or of a trick and it wears me out even more. You know how tired I arrive. Always. I try to brush aside the impatience that assails me because I fear, yes, my own reactions. The ferocity with which I could try to destroy the autonomy of your head.

I get up from the edge of the bed and go over to the small table and sit at the chair, my back to the bed, to you. I notice how annoyed I get at the stains on the wood. Today, yes, the stains, the crumbs, your face, the bread, affect my unstable spirits even more. I remove the notebook, the pencil, the glasses from my handbag. I lean over the page, smooth it out with the precise movement of my fingers before embarking on my habit with the numbers. I add, note down, distribute expenses on the page in an orderly fashion. I hear behind me, from the bed, your voice, your first words of the evening, turn on the light. I obey. I get up and turn on the light. I hadn't spotted how the room had darkened nor the effect of the dusk on my hand, on the notebook and on my hand-writing now almost faded on the contaminated page. Yes, contaminated by an identical fading in the columns of tightly-packed oscillating numbers. I examine the numbers under the light of the bulb. Then, after one final check, I close the notebook.

Turn off the light and come and lie down. It's already late, you whisper.

Controlling time and space proves to be essential. Ours, our time and our space. Keeping detailed track of each movement. You barely move at all. Not any more. But just the same, although you decided to surrender yourself to the bed, submitting yourself to the sheets, folding up, burying your head in the foam mattress, maintaining the same trousers forever, appeasing the circulation of your blood, reducing your heart rate, thinking with no correlate, you do in fact take care of yourself. You take care of your time and your space, you take care of me and, even more than that, you watch me. You keep control of my stay in the room. You wait, trusting, though pierced by a slight anxiety, always, for me to get into bed and in that way you can measure the pauses in my breathing or confirm the precise moment when I pass into sleep. Why watch me or watch you or watch us. We stay simply in our space in the most routine way possible, trying not to get out of joint. We live together and we polish our coexistence even more, although we are a cell that's completed and all used up, a cell that's dead. But without risk or with risk, that's something we cannot foresee, we persist.

A danger does exist, I know it.

Previously we used to proliferate in tens, always identical. Ten. The number made up part of an organic structure, of a cellular process. Ten. Not one more or one less. I can see them. I can see each one of our cells, wary, ordered, complete. I glimpse the most brilliant and executive cell we had, the one where our much-prized autonomy was consolidated. We belonged and we did not belong. We were a cell wandering between others, we knew it, other cells that were equally autonomous and threatened. We knew the cellular risk, one might sort of say we were experts, we knew how they worked, how they behaved. Then they declined, in a way one might say they fell sick. Our cell fell sick from an excess of arrogance and autonomy. You performed your role of womb or of mother, however you want to define it.

Our organicity. We ten bodies battled difficulties, we knew we were surrounded by other cells, pursued, entangled in our aliases. Mine, yours. My alias. I can't shit, you say to me, You can't? It's been three days, it's three already. Three days? A laxative, I'll go buy you a laxative. I don't know, you say to me, a laxative? Exactly, you could get sick. I know you're on the verge of getting sick from our routine and if you do get sick, well then what? We would have to, of course, go to the hospital, wait on the benches, present our doctored IDs, sit patiently till we're called, shuffle over to the emergency room, greet the doctor or not, surrender ourselves to the whim of the staff, to their careless manner, answer for you, describe your symptoms, enter the examination area, see the state of your organs on the monitor.

Keep quiet, watch, concede.

Listen from a distance to the diagnosis, wait for them to admit you while they grant you a bed, long for your death in the hospital. For you to die. Yes, die, once and for all. But no. Your intestines are playing a nasty trick on you. Always. Constipated. You hate shit, the smell, the texture, its wretchedness. You hold out, and hold out, to the point where you are approaching the threshold of paralysis and after a few days, at a given moment, you shut yourself in the bathroom to return worn out or overburdened or battered by the intestinal effort and then you sleep. It's part of a rite, three days of constipation, three days of rattling in order thus to restart the cycle. It is a debt you keep to yourself. Don't bother, you said to me, it's not your business, no, of course it isn't, but it bothers me, yes, the noises, your face slightly red, toxic, constipated, because it does bother you, doesn't it? Until in a real and solid space it stopped concerning me. I saw you just as you were, just like yourself. I watched you from the table on the days when I was doing some frantic sums, terrified of making a mistake with the numbers and, as I looked at you, I understood, with the violence and certainty of an enlightenment, that it was simply an obsession that was excessively realistic, all too human, already reported in many books of anatomy. I knew it. My protracted studies irritated you, you felt my curiosity distancing me from the factory-inclined consciousness to which you'd surrendered yourself. You were determined to define industrial behaviour and its variables. You wanted to fence in the symptoms and the ills of production. More than a cell, we resembled an amorphous research team. I told you this. I dared to express it because I'd heard it, I understood that a criticism of your attitudes had been unleashed which was received, that's how they put it, as a deviationism on your part. In those tense days, when most of the cells had already been brought down, when they'd been harassed and invaded and infiltrated, when they were falling or dying one after another, when they'd failed over and over in their objectives, you gave yourself the job or the luxury of beginning an assault on already exhausted industrial production. You made me go over my notes again, you charged me with a lengthy and sterile protocol that would bring the variables together. I wanted to say no. I even tried to, because the subject seemed to have been so voraciously explored already. I said this to you: we know it, we studied it, we analysed it, we drew conclusions, we did specialised courses, we worked through the night, we exploded the third cell.

Ah, that third cell, ten magnificent synchronised bodies all yearning. Ten desires. I fulfilled my functions, each one of us. We carried out a scientific exploration of the means of production, we noticed industrial flight and how it was transformed into a major crisis. We wore ourselves out. I worked non-stop writing a report that didn't end up convincing you because, you said, it had structural flaws.

I mocked.

That meeting went on for more than eight hours. I set out my results and limited myself to the report and to the heap of references on which I was basing my comments. The cell, the third one, began to collapse. Because, after all, who could have held out against pressure as monumental as the pressure you exerted. This crazy insistence on fencing in the means of production and the paradox of your refusing to accept the results. You didn't accept them because they went against the principles you had. After my exposition only one way out was left and the cell could see it coming. You got involved in a piece of meaningless rhetoric that called into question the most tangible reality of history. Today I can state that the isolation and the strong cell compartmentalisation exposed us to a space that was too empty, where reference points ended up disappearing. If you all get involved in this foolish theory people are going to die, you said. People have already died, I answered. It was conclusive. The third cell we formed went into a state of radical proliferation. We had to escape that cell and they, the eight who were left, faced with a spectacular industrial fall, turned to carrying out truly anarchist practices that left a considerable loss of human life in their wake. That cell was infected or infiltrated and we were about to fall. Us two. It led to a waste. The trail of blood left behind, its tangible, dismal traces. That cell, the third, trapped in the most confused and critical days was transformed into a model of extermination and of ultimate and incompressible destruction. (They're here, almost completely undone on the floor and in spite of their disastrous state they try to get into the bed with me, the third cell have not forgiven me yet.) Why talk, what use is it now, reckon up the losses or reconstruct the defeat, the successive and unmistakable defeat, you say. But were there triumphs?, I ask you, at least one victory?, which cell was successful or healthy?, in which space were we able to contribute?

That's how the history goes, you know this, slow and cruel, all massed together, you say or I think you say.

Now on this special day you are ready or available. Nothing troubles us and we can, with a truly enthusiastic attitude, re-do certain events. But we ought to be careful, to omit, to censor, thereby guaranteeing our survival. We need to keep our own acts clandestine, even faced with ourselves. This was the agreement, this the practice to which we surrendered. Not to say, never to name those facts that could end up incriminating us or giving us away or pushing us into a scrutiny that we do not desire. This silence, our silence, makes up a part of the secrets into which history is resolved. They have not yet discovered us, the successive, old cells that survived, because if they did, they would give themselves away. There are rumours, remarks, comments. Your name is circulating in nostalgic, private, or accusatory conversations, and not mine, no, not my name, our aliases.

Oh, if we talked, I say to you, if we said, do you realise, I say, what would happen in response to our statements, faced with the documents to which we can have recourse, do you realise how much we could obstruct or destroy, I don't know, the whole indulgent laxity of this time. We won't do it however, we won't do it. But if we talked, you know, we could bring disorder. You smile. I understand that the mere possibility prompts a flicker of vitality in you. You pull your hand out from under the blanket. My wrist hurts, kid, you say, and you move your hand to relax or decompress, I don't know, the joint. It hurts?, I say, is it the cold or the humidity or the betrayal of your bones or a stupid, unavoidable cycle of the wrist, the wrist, which wrist, *kid*, what a totally laughable word, they aren't going to transform me, I said, into one of those, it won't happen. No chance. Although we couldn't and shouldn't be personal, I forced myself to keep up a discussion with you, a conversation that could be considered personal, with our backs to the cell, sitting strategically in the room we occupied at the time. Who do you think you are, or any of you, I even said, after having noticed the irony that got unleashed while my intervention unfolded. An irony, don't deny it, don't do it, that was wounding and undeserved. That same irony that got tangled up in the word kid. He called me a kid, to destabilise me and thus to diminish an undeniable contribution.

It was your ally of the moment who did it, one-armed Juan.

He occupied his place with vigour, but, of course, without restraining himself and without the least possibility of concealment. I was right on the verge or in the moment, I don't know, of being chosen as cell chief of a body that could have become legend. When one-armed Juan said, this kid, he might even have said this little kid, I realised how my hopes were dashed on the rocks and there was nothing I could do but resign myself. But later, in the room, sitting opposite you, I managed to give vent

74

to my impressions. (At this moment one-armed Juan has that ironic look on his face, leaning up against the wall opposite our bed, the wall is stained and one-arm's face is downcast, impossible, hazy.)

Oh, so your wrist hurts, does it, kid?, how much?, how much does it hurt, kid?, how does it hurt?, describe in great detail your symptoms, the axis of the pain, the way of moving about, yes, the pain, which bone exactly, which ligament in your hand, which rotation you're capable of performing, can you, by any chance, turn your wrist, how badly affected are your fingers. Answer in order. You blink as if by moving your eyelids you could memorise or as if the possibility of retention resided in your eye. You shake your head and sink into the pillow. Your arm has disappeared hidden by the blanket. You don't want to any more. You go back to being the lump that houses you best. I must, I know, return to confront the numbers arranged on the page. I can feel them turning hostile, the numbers, feel them pursuing me relentlessly to reveal their total. Oh, numbers and their infinite boasting, their stupid science or their abstract, calligraphic art. I could get hold of a calculator, but you're against it. You said no to the calculator, no, because it would injure us with its technology, you said no to anything technical and I, of course, understood how far your refusal went or how your refusal about the calculator converted into a word that was coming to bring redemption, for us both.

I could perhaps pity you, I did it, I pitied myself and forgot. I rejected the television, we gave up. We did not want to be trapped by its tendency and its flow.

How many?, how many years? (a thousand years): more than a century, of course.

Wearily you take up the discontinued newspaper, and we read its pages at a distance. We know how charismas and reputations are constructed. We see certain photos and the names that are printed there for ratification. We recognise those names and their affiliations. At one point you shook your head stunned with surprise and confusion. You looked at the photo in the paper, you read the page and sank in further still. But not any more. We don't get surprised and even more we look serenely at how these faces are possessed. They are printed on the pages, far away now from any cell. There they are. But now I look at the photograph I keep between the pages of the notebook. We are posing confidently before the camera with our backs to the sea that's visible in the background. I am holding the little boy in my arms while you stroke his head. Small, beautiful, a delicate thing. A wonderful sea stretches out behind us, a sea that is there to ratify the power of the ocean. The three of us are, you and me and the boy, far from any interference. It was the only trip to the sea we took with the boy, and we were scared, fearful of an action that was so impetuous. Oh, if we'd drowned in those waters. (They say that we drowned in the waters, that we left no trace.) Backs to the sea, the boy you and me, the three of us in a photo that has become obsolete.

A photo, the only one, confirming him, the boy.

I get up with the photo in my hand, I want to show you the photo, the one we know so well, the picture we go to when reality loses any consistency or else in the most intense moments of nostalgia or in rage or within the narrow margins of pity that we allow ourselves. I sit down with the photo on the narrowest edge of the bed. I search for your hand beneath the blanket to put it onto the photo. Your fingers run over the paper.

Does it hurt?, I ask you, does your wrist hurt, kid?

Yes, you answer me, your voice distorted by the breathlessness that your blanket-hidden head causes you.

Yes, you say to me again, it still hurts.

I experience an unmistakeable feeling of wellbeing very close to forgetting or to the desire to remain suspended in an immovable iron present. I see how you, meanwhile, get immediately lost in yourself. You could, in reality, yes, walk on your own, with that treacherous way you have of dragging your feet, of spreading the traces of the pain caused by the calamitous state of your legs, that habit of lowering your head, imprinting a pronounced curve onto your spine. You are alone surrendered to a kind of impenetrable absence that passes through the obstinate neutrality of your face. We do the same route, the usual one. Tiny, precise. Surrounded by the dusk, we turn the corner, then walk the two blocks that take us to the square. We cross it. Your eyes never come to rest on the bodies already obscured by the shadows, quite unreal, nor do you notice unexpected details like the sudden opening of a new grocery store, a little one, so small that it hardly fits within its own interior. You don't see it or you notice it only tangentially or you don't want me to notice that you've seen it because any gesture might oblige you to share an amazement that's irrelevant and you don't do that, because you've surrendered to the autonomy of remoteness, the remoteness that's a part of the slow monthly walk, yours, ours, always.

We cross over, leave the square behind, walk in a straight line into the last street of ours, always the same one, this street marked by the instability of the paving stones that obliges us to look out for the cracks so as not to trip. You don't want to trip and your watchful eyes focus on the flaws in the cement and, at once, you take my arm, very near the elbow, the right, and I feel how, in a way, you squeeze it too tight, thus avoiding me being the one who stumbles. You don't want, you protect, you repel, through the pressure of your hand, me to lose my balance and to lean chaotically on you. You can't stand it, you don't like being touched unexpectedly, nobody, you've said, you do it, you protect yourself. I feel your fingers very near my elbow and it's as though my arm has expanded till it doesn't belong to me any more or else has reduced me to the only thing that defines me, an arm. I'd like to say to you, let go of my arm or I can't bear you touching my arm or get your hand off my arm, but I say nothing hoping that this disastrous street will end, without picking up the pace so you won't notice in what way and how much this decision of yours to obstruct bothers me. The pavement is impossible as if the mere abstract addition of a day might ruin it even more. Like the unleashing of a minuscule nuclear attack, its ancient surface has already become collapsed. I register you burying your fingers even deeper into my arm and I am assailed by a feeling that repels me because in squeezing me you are revealing my arm to me, the whole thing, yes, an arm on which I do not want to linger and to which, nonetheless, I walk chained like a deadweight.

Then we head towards our street, you release my arm. We have only a few minutes left, how many, three, five, perhaps. Three or five minutes of air, enough for you to lose patience and wish our arrival would hurry up, I know it, because your steps intensify, their rhythm rises slightly and your face takes on a worried expression until the urgency that passes across the lines of your eyes takes shape.

Albeit sidelong, I see you.

I understand you want to go back into the room once

and for all so as to conclude a ritual that already weighs you down incredibly, and which means nothing. But I don't give in. I hold firm and I do not change the rhythm of my steps, I remain impassive, far removed from your longings, because I want the minutes to pass fully, each one, without avoiding them, with no possible renunciation. You accept and you surrender to the final stretch. You reduce your steps, shorten them. It is a fleeting time, you've understood that, so short that you give in and allow me to enjoy myself. I feel, of course I do, the cold air on my face, on my legs. Only on my face and on my legs because my overcoat, the usual one, the one in dark wool, is protecting me. I am assailed by an unstoppable desire to ask you if you are cold, are you cold?, I ask you in spite of myself. Yes. I supposed as much, but it's benign, benign, nothing now might spoil the linear sliding by of the minutes, nothing. You came out, of course, without a coat, you always do, as if you wanted to put your own endurance to the test or perhaps to explore within your body the signs of a slight adversity. But now this final time belongs to me, it's mine and I know it has come to an end because we're entering the house, opening the door to the room and you go straight to the stove and light it. I see you crouched in front of the stove, I hear the rough, efficient sound of the match, I notice the smell of paraffin, unmistakeable, which necessarily produces a vague but persistent headache in me, yet it remains inevitably there, the smell, expanding. You straighten up until you're standing in front of the stove, you rub your hands to get more heat, more. I put my overcoat away in the little closet, I hang it from the hook. I get out the biscuits and a bar of chocolate. I put the chocolate and the biscuits on top of the table, I know that's my part: the kitchen, the kettle, the cups, the sugar, our bodies face to face at the table that's so small, so small.

You take the chocolate and divide it equitably. We like chocolate a lot, me more, more, its taste, that slow eager wandering across the gums, across the concave palate, I never bite it, never, rather I let it come apart in my mouth until my saliva soaks it up and I prolong the moment when it slides down my throat. You, meanwhile, take your bit of chocolate fast, you're hungry and immediately afterwards you take one of the biscuits which crunch under your crashing teeth. I look away, I don't want to interfere in those overblown sounds of yours and that's why I look at the floor and notice, at once, that the floorboards need waxing, the time's come, you've got to wax them because how long has it been since last time you had a go with the scouring wool, the thickest I could find, you did it bad-temperedly, loading all your weight onto the scourer to extract from the floorboards all the unpleasant sticky accretions that had ended up as substantial built-up dirt. Then, you collapsed, appreciably diminished, you had to lie down drained in bed. I thought you wouldn't be able to continue with the floor wax, but you did it. Then I took charge of the polishing, the following day, but that night was hard, I slept intermittently pierced by the smell of wax surrounding us and I told you in the morning, the smell, I talked to you about my toxic concern. Then you looked at me with an ironic glimmer, comic even, I knew that with your lips oscillating between a grimace and the sharpness of a smile, you were saying it was my fault, the wax, the smell, your getting worn down. You were saying to me, by means of this grimace smile, that you were the real victim of an idiotic decision and in that way you were underlining your own total indifference to the declining state of the floorboards.

I look up again.

You're going to have to wax the floor, I say, very quickly, yes.

For a moment, your mouth freezes, you stop chewing the biscuit, you shut your eyes, you take a breath, filled with astonishment, and you get up from the table. You go out to the bathroom briefly and come back. You stay behind, prowling the room, you lean on the wall and then you approach the bed and sit down, as usual, your head in your hands. I don't look at you, I'm presuming all this. I go on as if you were still there, I pretend nothing has happened, that at any moment you're going to sit down again, but a certain troubled feeling begins to incubate, a feeling of abandonment or of hostility or of shame that stops me eating the biscuit, the one I'd already removed from the packet. I set the biscuit down on the plate, I get up and take the handbag off the nail, I sit back down at the table, I put on my glasses and look for my notebook. But I understand in advance that there's nothing new on the pages because the accounts are in order, but I do need to pretend I'm carrying out a task so as to avoid the feeling of total foolishness filled with rage that assails me. I can't make out the individual numbers in the notebook clearly, I've got to strain my eyes to check the working days, the exact hours, I really must switch to a new pair of spectacles, that's something I need vitally and so do you. Your eyes no longer respond to you, I've noticed it when you're reading, you take off your glasses and press your eyelids every once in a while or bring the pages nearer or move them further or you end up, disappointed, giving up on your reading. I experienced a sudden shyness the time you asked me to read you the instructions for the medicine, the weight of a feeling dropped between us, something like humility or an extensive compassion. You just couldn't make out the letters. Clumsily, but quite necessarily, I laughed. You can't see anything any more, I said, you need to change your glasses. Yes, yes, you whispered, yes, just to appease. You understood, you did, that we were affected, that we were obliged to share.

Sitting at the table now, I would like to cancel the whole stupid business with the wax, to go back completely and pick up the biscuit again, but it's too late because you won't forgive me for pushing you into a space you can't stand, the one, in reality, that you hate in me. I see you at this moment stretched out on the bed, soon you'll get between the sheets to set out towards the night.

I get up, go over to the bed and hand you the packet of biscuits. Eat, I say. You take the packet and its metallic paper crackles noisily. Have them all yourself, I say. I sit down on the edge of the bed and I go back over the magazine, the one I already know, I just let the time pass turning pages of no importance. I know that while you eat, you are watching me, that it brings you relief, after all, that I'm there, that I'm able to turn the pages in silence, I feel you expanding in the bed, I feel you moving, safe and, in a way, comforted simply because we exist. After a period I cannot determine, I realise that it's time, that we will definitely need to surrender together to the night.

I walk over to the cupboard, I fold my clothes on the chair and put on my nightie. At that moment, I turn out the stove, switch off the light and get into bed. I climb across the bed till I find myself in the corner, beside the wall and after some clumsy movements, I arrange myself until I'm slotted in with your body. I feel I am immersed in a fake darkness, since I'd still be able to define each one of the corners, as if the bedroom were infested with light or as if the objects never stopped because they had been imprinted on the backs of my eyelids. I fight to distance the images, to get away from the precision with which the room is ordered outside my head. Within my closed eyes I have the whole room wounding me with its disturbing clarity, I know it's a visual disturbance, a simple trick of the light and that it will very soon fade away. I withdraw from my own eyes and allow the necessary moments to go by in order for the troubling effect to be eliminated.

Slowly I turn my back and I push you, I push you so that you move onto the most radical extremes of your side, move over, I say to you, and you do it. In that way I'm able to rest my spine in a more human position. My spine bothers me, the bones hurt in sync, in a symmetrical chain that never stops, the pain identical to the perfect sketch of the joints, an involuntary complaint escapes me and you try to reduce yourself further still. I don't know if you do it because the complaint irritates you or out of sympathy. But you retreat with the submissiveness I know in you and which bothers me so much, a domestic pet, scared, obedient, servile, a dog. You're aware of my back, I'm aware how hard you find it getting to sleep, how you lie there rigid, waiting.

Night is always difficult, bed always relentless.

I turn around and now I'm the one who prefers being on my side, the great work of the bones. Then you move, subtly, following me, as if we were protagonists in some protracted horizontal ballet, the people chosen to carry out a wayward dance.

Always monotonous; the night and the bed.

Our legs have no choice but to adjust in a kind of imperative and harmonious dialogue. I feel the brush of your rough trousers on my legs and with a quick movement I pull down my nightie to prevent it. I'd like to let myself fall, fall towards sleep, right now. But once again I need to move. How much time's passed between one movement and the next, could it have been an hour, I wonder, while I feel the heat of your foot, too stuck to mine, to my naked foot which, at the encounter with yours, is starting to transform into a bone centre that's as active as my spine was before if not more so, and at just the moment when I start to turn it from the sole you ask me if I saw the little grocer's, did you see it, you say to me, the one they've just opened, the new grocer's. No, I answer you with my face so close to the wall I can practically feel it pressed to my mouth, I didn't see it. And it's as if your words are circulating in space without having the hateful barrier of the wall, freer, and more, I don't know, more spacious, while I register how you are starting to turn your back, in a position that, no, no, no, that is mine.

Turn around.

There are no shadows or silhouettes. We like it. We never leave the window open because we need total darkness to sleep. It's just that I'm experiencing an increased sensitive aversion to light. You turn around and your head is very close to mine, I feel your breath on my neck filtering through my hair. Your knees and my knees, your feet and my feet. My back and your chest. I feel, too, that I am on my way out, that the wished-for sleep is starting to become concrete, I know you don't want me to sleep, that you'd rather I kept you company in your wakefulness, but it's not up to me, not even I am still up to me because from some imprecise but conclusive moment our bodies begin to fade away, to fade away. And in the final seconds of foggy consciousness that I have left, I notice how the bed withdraws until it ceases at last to support us.

After covering his back with the blanket, I move him slowly to the bathroom. Even on his own he is capable of performing a tight little sliding movement keeping his feet practically stuck to the floor. I decide not to get annoyed at the slowness. I lean him against the wall. When I have seen that there is sufficient brightness filtering through the window, I turn on the shower. I take the blanket off him and fold it on the chair. I look for the shampoo, the soap and the sponge. I manage to get his pyjama top off easily, though I understand that the major stumbling block will lie in the bottoms and his refusal to lift his feet. I know him. But I know how to get him to lift his legs. I pull down his plastic underpants, I undo the fasteners and rummage between his legs, remove the urine-soaked diaper. I wrap the diaper and take it to the rubbish bin, then drop the pyjamas and underpants into the laundry basket.

We're ready, I say to him, let's get into the water.

I don't want to, he says.

Remember today's the day we have a bath, I answer him. Let's have our bath, I insist.

No, no, no, he says.

He's crying. Like every Thursday he has started to cry and the features of his face blur with that massive grimace squeezing it. I take one of the paper tissues and dry his tears. He is sobbing openly, standing up, naked, his arms hanging limp at his sides. Fearful that he might totter and fall, I take him by the shoulders.

We're just going to have a quick bath, nice and quick, I say.

No, no, he says.

But I can see him giving way now and allowing me to help him with his legs. First one, then the other. I check the temperature of the water. I sit him on his bath seat, ready for the washing. The water is warm, bountiful. I soak the sponge with the soap and proceed to run it over his chest. I see how thin he's become, his ribs marked out clearly on his skin, foretelling the exact dimension of his skeleton. I soap his genitals and I can't stop myself looking for a moment at his now practically non-existent legs that are rapidly approaching a dangerous undernourishment.

I squat down so I can reach his feet with the sponge. The water scatters when it strikes the cap and the plastic of the smock covering me. And that's the moment he lifts his leg to knee me full in the face. A blow of such magnitude that I experience a universal explosive sensation in the bone of my nose. I fall. I struggle up into a sitting position on the bathroom floor. There on the ground I press my nose with both hands in indescribable pain. I curl up. The pain climbs until it consumes my head and encloses me or blinds me while I rock back and forth to lessen it, to dislodge the hatred that passes in parallel to the movement of the pain across my whole head, my face and the base of my neck. At some considerable distance from the pain, I hear the noise of the water, as it falls copiously onto the stool while I surrender to the physical horror of the bathroom floor. I remain seated, leaning on the tiled wall, moments or minutes waiting surrendered to thousands or millions of piercing darts, praying for the pain to abate, squeezing my nose. It moves about, expands, intensifies in some areas. I remain like this, sitting on the floor, reduced to a suffering fragment of bones until I realise how the density of the pain is starting to slip away, yes, its power is decreasing as the chaotic reality of the water rises up before me.

My nose throbs. Then I take my hands from my face and I find myself again.

Uncertainly, I get to my feet. I'm afraid the pain might reappear, that this is a fake truce. I gently dry my flushed face with the towel and go over to the mirror. I can see that a conspicuous swelling has appeared at the bridge of my nose. Still standing in front of the mirror, I straighten the cap and return to the water. I already feel like I'm ready to handle the pain. I bend over the bottom of the tub till I'm able to retrieve the soap and the sponge. I straighten up and, careful not to catch his eye, lift him, rub his back and his almost non-existent buttocks. My nose is still throbbing at a similar rhythm, as if the echo of the pain had imposed a memory through some scientific chronology. I lower him back onto the seat. I take the shampoo. I tilt his head and notice how much the allergy has advanced, manifest in a series of soft lumps that practically cover his whole head. Psoriasis, I think. It's consuming him, I think. The same psoriasis that is implacably assailing his genitals and which allows him no peace, dragging him into a protracted insomnia. I see the insomnia in his ravaged features now that we're face to face and I dry those lines with the towel. I bring the towel up to his head and rub it. The movement relieves his constant itching which is why he raises his hand and takes the towel. I allow him to move it himself a little, then I lift his hands off his head and hurriedly dry his body. I help him with his feet, I put on his bathrobe and cover his back with the blanket and guide him to his room again, even with the acute limitations of his steps.

My nose is still throbbing intermittently, like a simple reminder. I touch the swollen area and I fear that in a few hours I'm going to have black eyes. I take off his bathrobe and the blanket. I lie him on his back on the bed, spread his legs, take the cream and apply it to his genitals. The allergy has even invaded the lower part of his stomach and the edges of his hips. I hear him murmur unconnected words while trying to scratch, but I stop him so that the cream can get through his skin and bring him some relief. I take the diaper out of the dresser drawer and arrange it on him, then I move onto the clean plastic underpants I'd previously left on the bed. I hold him by his arms and raise him off the bed.

Time for us to get dressed, I say to him.

He does not collaborate and forces me to rotate his arms to insert them into the sleeves of the shirt. Then I confront the task of putting his trousers on while struggling with his feet and the stubborn resistance he offers me.

Let's lift our feet up just a bit now. Just a bit, I say to him.

After several, difficult movements I have finished dressing him. He's standing, weakened now, expressionless. I sit him in his wheelchair and go back into the bathroom to fetch a comb. I return to the bedroom and comb his hair. He can't stop his hands trembling. His legs are trembling, too. Yet his absent expression does convey a curious kind of fullness. But I mustn't deceive myself, having made one unforgivable mistake, I know I must remain alert now because at any moment he might attack me and then the look in his eyes will attain that glint of rejection I know, emerging from somewhere that is still intact, ready to destroy. Now he scratches his head, clumsily, irregularly, messing his neatly combed hair. I realise I haven't put the cream on. I get the pot, scoop out some cream, and use my fingers to spread it on his head, affected by the irregularity of the rashes that stretch from the end of his forehead to the back edge of his neck.

Then I take the comb and once again tidy the straggling remnants of hair that poke out from his skull. I bend down to put on his socks and shoes. I arrange his shirt, and straighten his trousers, then leave him sitting in the chair while I go back to the bathroom. There I put the comb away in the drawer, and take off the smock and cap. I examine my face in the mirror. Yes, I do have a swollen nose. I'd rather not look. I put on my dress, my tights, my coat. I put the cap and smock away in my bag and return to the bedroom.

One of his feet is hanging off the wheelchair. I squat down to arrange it on its footrest. With a well-timed manoeuvre, I dodge the vague smack he launches at my head. I had anticipated it. I straighten up and take a good look at him.

He's dying, I think to myself.

In the middle of a dream that is entirely taken over by the sound of bullets and amazing fireworks exploding in unison, bullet and firework resound, as if in an amplified litany, the unfinished sentence: 'Constant revolutionising of production, uninterrupted disturbance of all social conditions, everlasting uncertainty and agitation...' The dream, threaded through with images that are fragmentary, contradictory and incoherent: remnants of bodies, irreplaceable organs, faces that are distant yet constantly loved, bone avalanches in an evident state of war. A dream that does not quite turn into a nightmare but is, nonetheless, troubling. A boy on his feet, totally exposed. I wake up just to try to understand the images. I wake up, this time, with a mission that consists of trying to dislodge the chaos to restore an equally ruinous but, at least, more understandable structure. In reality I wake up to resettle myself in the bed and to emerge from a dream that, I know full well, could never be resolved because it pertains to an enigmatic sphere that persists for ever. I have emerged from the dream to find myself in pain and obviously stiff. I'm aware of the damage to my hand from its unacceptable position in the bed. My hand. I need my hand, it's of use to me, and yet, it could get injured and be put out of circulation. It is the circulation, the blood blocked by the hand's position on the bed. The blood could stop its flowing and its dizziness just to disable me, leaving me inactive with my hand dead, bloodless, my hand done for, facing what we fear so much, the decline into an unproductive life. A hand without vital signs, like you, like you. You look like a dead man in the bed, heavy, watery, trapped in rigidity. But you are breathing definitively. You aren't dead, what am I thinking, you're asleep as if you were dead or you're alive as if you were dead or you're alive as if they'd murdered you on one of those streets guarded by technological eyes tipped off by the indiscriminate growth in cells that are impossible to stabilise. Murdered on the public street or in one of the emergency rooms, altogether dead, bloody and visceral, with legs broken and guts dangling, strung up on the most well-guarded street and one of your eyes flying towards the sidewalk, an anxious eye on the chapped cement, dead.

You are breathing, alive, lying in the bed, on the night when I wake up, right now, crippled on the piece of the uneven mattress that hurts me, hurts my whole damn essential spine and which has now ended up, that mattress, assaulting my curled-up hand, my hand aches, I can't open my hand, I say to you, help me, I ask you, what?, what hand are you saying?, the right, the right, I complain. You sit up in bed and try to open my hand. No, no, don't touch me, don't you dare, open my hand or cut off my hand or I don't want my hand or I've had enough, enough of all this discomfort, mine or yours, in this endless bed that's either shoddy or it's plastic foam, sunken and perverse this foam, this damned bed, its mattress recycled through enormous industrial waste. Don't talk, don't keep on about industry and its vertiginous collapse, what is it you're trying to achieve?, maybe you're trying to destroy. No, I answered you, no, this is a political action, a productive reformulation, generating, I told you, a more up-to-date scenario, starting to read again, to think, it's about taking a decision, intervening in our times. Killing, you said to me, Stalinist, because what you're looking for is an explosion that's impossible to carry out. They're dying like flies. As soon as I said flies, I knew I'd used an expression that was stupid or sterile, a bad conjunction, an, of course, inevitably, frightening commonplace that would prove to be unfavourable.

You laughed.

You had a face, at that moment, that was really striking, those teeth, that mouth, the nose, the large forehead. A face, truly, that was inescapably material, that set human craftsmanship in relief. My eyes roamed your face and because of this, because of the intensity of my scrutiny, I didn't pause at the insult that was contained within your laugh, I didn't go back over that already known term Stalinist, I was alert only to the inner workings of your features and to a mystical flicker that assailed me when I thought about human craftsmanship while I looked at the total effect of your face while you were laughing and you were laughing because you already knew or understood or foresaw that we were lost, that our cell, the last one of all, would be wrecked by the imperatives of what we so feared, of history. We had one cell left, the last one, when our time was crumbling away and you precisely chose to laugh, you laughed at the moments when the whole last leadership of the party had fallen, you laughed when the infiltration was irrefutable, you laughed as if you were not a militant and I, I must admit, I focused on your face, not on your laughing, on the totally crazy shape of your face, the sculptural precision of your features, and I allowed myself, yes, I allowed myself a few inappropriate reflections that were verging on the worst human sentimentality, because on this occasion, possessed as I was, I reached the edge, I let myself fall into an awkward and unforgivable abyss that pushed me to wonder about the possibility of the existence of a God.

My deviationism was due to your face, to the most visible aspect of human organisation, the face, I mean, as an indestructible sign, as a singularity, not yours, not your specific one, rather the traditional symbol of one, of the always unrepeatable face. Because of those thoughts I now recognise as stupid, I put all that drivel to one side, your drivel, which classified me as a Stalinist, a definition that appeared at those moments when the cells were going to stop and between them, ours already invaded and infiltrated by little Maureira, that really short guy who collaborated left, right and centre with the reformist groups, the same little runt whose face would later pop out of the photograph in the paper and both of us shut our eyes in shock or terror at seeing Maureira without his alias, now reconverted into Javier Montes, that's right, all totally above-board now, proud to show off his name in the paper, the runt who switched sides, at just the right moment, when it was still possible and who didn't hesitate to weaken our cell to secure his own place in a history that – we saw it, we experienced it, we suffered it – was not going to get anywhere or would drop anchor at exactly the productive stage some of us had predicted.

And you, of course, you're wrong, you got it wrong, didn't you?, I say, as I try to move my hand a bit to loosen it up, you called me a Stalinist, making yourself part of a mistake that now sees us lying on this tiny mattress, amid a foam that's toxic, so toxic, as toxic as paraffin or history, as toxic as the imminent death of the boy in the bed, we need to get him out, take him to hospital, shut up, you say to me, don't go on, don't go on, while I sit on the bed, rocking myself as if I were a baby, yes, a needy child, in those unspeakable days when hospitals did not have the capacity to hold back an infection, the boy ever more feverish, his bronchi oppressed and confused, panting, seeking some empty space in his body to be able to breathe and get relief. I felt it, that unbearable, guttural, unmistakable noise and you, I know, you understood it just the same as me, that we needed to take him to hospital, to disguise ourselves in order to get seen. Go at night, out onto the street with the boy in our arms, look for something in which to transport ourselves, risking ourselves and then arriving with the boy in our arms at the hospital and managing to get some attention that might do away with the deadly sounds that day by day, through this awful week, were deepening and not responding to my care, I covered him, lulled him to sleep, kissed him, looked at him, gave him his medicines one by one, measured the progress of his fever rigorously and scientifically, wanted you to die, not the boy, no not the boy, you've got to die and then I could go with the boy, both disappear, the boy and me, and we'd leave you dead in the room like a dog, but us, me and the boy, we'd survive, we'd get away from the hell of your face and away from the hell that you thought without respite that the boy was a product of the horror, of the madness, that the boy was a flaw, my flaw, my pig-headedness, a malicious understanding of history that brought our militant duty tumbling to the ground.

Why didn't you die?

Shut up, you say to me.

Ah, if you'd died, no, not the boy, and my amazing, irresponsible weakness, how many blocks away was the hospital, within what range, what were its facilities like, what staff were on shift that night, how up-to-date was its technology, how many beds should it have had available for emergencies, what were the exact quality and objective capacity of the ventilators, what was going on with the oxygen, did children die that night?, the emergency, the shifts, the oxygen canisters. A hospital bed, metallic and small, small, the room vast, the arid beds, the inhibited breathing, the children dying that night, but not mine, never in the hospital bed, far removed from the oxygen, from the intravenous drip, from the essential and foul-smelling antibiotics, from the overalls and the whole impressive process of sterilisation. The paraffin, it was the paraffin, don't you think?, I ask you. Shut up. But what was to be done when faced with the total cold, I put water and herbs on top of the stove, I waited for the steam that would relieve the frightening, alarming smell of paraffin, that smell that made him worse, that set about destroying first his chest, don't cough, don't cough, let me sleep, how much longer are you smoking in the room, I say to you, always, half crazed by the interruption of my sleep, you cough like some consumptive from another century, yes, the paraffin that was progressively destroying his two lungs, both of them, the total accumulation of phlegm in his lungs until it put an end to the indispensable beatings of his small, beloved, heart.

I turned off the stove, risking the cold because the fever had already taken control of his body, fever inside and out, he was burning, I swear he's burning and I asked you, then, for wet cloths, soak the towel and bring it over, quick, hurry, I said to you, soak it through and then you wring it out into the bathtub. We wrapped him in the wet towel, our hands were trembling, we'd hit the most crucial moment of the terror, the menace of that wet towel, its risks, putting onto a small child, so small, two years old, and feverish, a wet towel, putting it on in the most crucial hours of his inevitable death, undressing the boy, wrapping him in a towel that's worn, wet, maybe pervaded by the contamination, onto a boy who was catching fire with fever, who coughed at the smell of paraffin, who was writhing in the dawn of what would be death, ours, our irreversible death. My hand is maddening me, crooked and cramped, asleep, dead.

My hand.

I can't feel my hand, you say. Now it's you and your hand. Give it to me, I answer, give me your hand. I can't, I can't move it. You're cramping, I say, it's because of the sugar, it's the sugar, you know, I read it, I know it, I'm sure, no more sugar, I say, it's over, no more sugar, I insist. My hand, I can't feel it. You're terrified in the night and so you wake me in order to confirm the presence of your hand. That you have it, that you haven't lost it yet. You can't feel it, I say, because you slept in an awkward position, don't be alarmed, don't be alarmed, it'll pass soon enough, I tell you as I massage your hand, I start to return it to you and you relax and sigh and feel that maybe you should have done it, you should have done it yourself, managed to revive your hand. I don't want to take your hand during the night, never. I cannot feel your fingers let alone join our palms and nor could you have borne it, I know that, you cannot endure it and that is why, when you are able vaguely to move your fingers, you draw your hand apart and turn your back on me in a way that's disgraceful and evidently contemptuous and I turn, of course, towards the wall, the wall that's there, immovable, rigid, reliable. Those hands, I think, the ludicrousness of hands joined when partially triumphant, we used to take each other's hands at the sound of The Internationale, its music, its words that are so eloquent or persuasive, a mythical line-up of elated bodies that are young, so young and already shackled to The Internationale as we sealed an urgent commitment to history and you sang and I struggled to fix the song's words in my mind, I didn't want to get them wrong, it was dangerous, yes, changing a single word or a syllable within those great, sparkling lines and transforming the song, The Internationale no less, into trouble, demolishing it utterly to rubble.

There they were, the historic leaders, I could see them lined up along a not especially evocative stage.

The construction of the setting bothered me. I told them afterwards, mentioned that they needed to create a set design that was in keeping with the prestige of The Internationale. I pointed it out in a way that could have been considered irresponsible. It was merely an opinion or a tangential comment. But you and part of the group who would later make up the second cell replied too emphatically. Aristo, you called me, or bourgeois, I don't know, I'm not sure, I can't pin down the word now. But there was an arid platform, the leaders' bodies, the tune, the hands, the singing. The party leadership forming a depressing line on that impossible stage, all fused together and undifferentiated, they looked like regular militants, not leaders, not that at all, and meanwhile you really shone in the singing and fat López shone and Ximena and maybe even I shone (fat López, from a corner of the room is now denying the whole scene shaking his head, pale, furious, but I no longer care, oh how pale fat López looks while Ximena's talking to me, insisting on my murder, lying next to me, whispering it in my ear, in secret). No, I was not shining, I don't think so, that's not how I was, owing to my concentration and my panic at getting it wrong, amid some miserable little lights that had transformed the leaders into common, simple human beings, into men you might run into just around the corner, those corners that would later be transformed into fatal traps, for rats, no, no, for dogs, for dogs.

I want to sleep, it's late.

I rest my sleeping hand against the wall and feel nothing. I no longer feel anything at all.

You had already been through two, three, four schools for cadres, you had transformed into a cadre yourself, one of the best. That news was going around and, despite clandestinity, it was known or we knew that your achievements were going to bring you considerable expectations. Your circumstances were changing, allowing you to deal directly with the leaders, you alone were leaving the cell to hold certain private or privileged meetings with members of the party leadership. With them you feigned an appearance that, in the form of rumours or a not too subtle attempt at slander, made itself felt from cell to cell: the accusation of acting in a way that was driven by voluntarism. The party leadership, among those who would later be wiped out (they wander around, bad-tempered, tense, watching us with irritation), sought to put your total commitment to their lines, their agreements, their pacts, to the test. You assented, you conceded, you showed yourself almost too submissive, to an alarming degree. But inside, in the room, the one where we were living in those days, you were developing, I know it, I'm very well aware, a stringent study that pointed towards a reformulation of the fundamentals. We had been transformed into professionals in clandestinity, we knew how to move about, which routes to use to conceal ourselves, how to prowl around spaces, to dodge, to dodge the city and mitigate the impact of our bodies on the streets. I took your part, I supported you, you filled me with mistrust.

But I protected you.

I had transformed into a no, no, not ever officialised lieutenant. I commented on your analyses, because after all I had my own arsenal, my undisputed and memorable progress through each one of the cadre schools, my own prestige as an analyst, a whole protracted intense experience in the field of linguistics and my scientific training in the study of history. I told you, I did tell you, didn't I? Oh, you answered and I don't know why your exclamation gratified me. I am sitting at the table, digressing, before surrendering myself to settling the state of the numbers, our accounts, the impeccable columns of expenses, all of them, each one of them. You turn your back on me to demonstrate your indifference or your indolence towards my daily task. The expenses. I remember that I went out, in a totally foolish act, breaking with any logic of safety. I went out, walked along the pavements, exposing my already openly deformed appearance. And suddenly I experienced the impact of that dress which, though I refused to acknowledge it, occupied my desires completely and took control of my mind in secret waves of longing. The dress that made me stop walking and brought me face to face with the shop window and, all of a sudden, I wanted it, I wanted it, I adored it, I fell instantly in love. Its fabric, the way it hung, its design and the urgent, crazed need to buy the dress, put it on, flaunt it on myself, to consume the dress, devour it completely, to spend on the fabric, on the design, on the hang, surrender myself shamelessly, with not the tiniest flicker of guilt, to a bacchanalian and absolute pleasure at ostentation, the most harmful space in which my body could ever end up. Renouncing the renunciation we had made in the early years when we took refuge once and for all behind a consistent contempt.

I struggled to take off the bulging trousers, the

shapeless blouse, the vest, to burn them, destroy them in the devastating power of a bonfire and go blindly or virginally towards the dress to be reborn or revived or to avoid a destiny marked by the total excess of body, by the absence of outlines, a body that had experienced naked or real history, a history that through its whole vast time always went out of its way to destroy. We took it on, we assumed the immovable direction of a frugality that was truly militant, austere, both of us, your austerity, my austerity.

Except that day.

What had happened that day?, what happened to me or happened to us to shackle me to the alienation of a cosmetic and reprehensible shop window?, what occurred within me to make me stop and surrender to a loathsome desire that broke the stoniest quality of my bones? The image of the dress weakened them and, in a way, scorned them: my bones did this to my bones. My hungry look, a desire that exploded unexpectedly, that broke boundaries, each one of the strategies I needed or we needed to construct, and which enabled some bones to spin like fragments towards the most extraordinary alienation. Yes, I, myself, a specialist in linguistics and totally aware of rejection as a process that was imperative and liberating, found myself before a shop window that was summoning me towards a tortuous dress designed to seduce and to flee from the avatars of a history, a dress that was going to liberate me from disgrace, that was going to distract me from a power that had finally pierced me down to the marrow of my bones. Yes, a power that had offended the only consistency of the body that we knew to be fundamentally bony.

And it is, because it bears some bones, some hard, hard bones, which are there to support it when faced with crises, one after another, the cells were falling, yes, one by one until I fell too, the first, and you fell, later, of course, and we both found ourselves confronted with the most savage and most intense experience that can possibly put militant resistance to the test.

But what happened that day?, that day when my bones weakened at the sight of something so derisory and wretched as a fabric and a design that after all are lurking in every one of the shop windows at which, oh no, no, we never stopped because we understood their structure and the power from which they emanated, the transparency of the glass, yet which in a baffling minute opened up within me the horizon of a desire we had proscribed because we understood or I understood, with the conviction befitting a qualified analyst, that behind each one of the shop windows lay the expansive ghost of a domination that crushed even the toughness of bones, that ground bones down in order to allow the triumph of an avid flesh, insatiable in the shop windows, this contingent flesh, captive and alienated and ready to turn its back on history and on the extraordinary, majestic materialism of bones. What happened?, I ask myself, I ask you, at that moment, that exact day, how could I have forgotten the line, the motto, the slogan, the illumination of a concept I knew or which my bones recited without hesitation, without a pause, without the least stammer: 'the bourgeoisie has through its exploitation of the world market given a cosmopolitan character to production and consumption in every country.'

How could I have dared to abandon my bones at that shop window?

What happened?, what happened?, I ask you.

When?, when?, you answer me.

The dress, for goodness' sake, the dress.

Which dress?, you say.

You say it with your back to me, turned towards

the wall, my wall, the one that belongs to me owing to the position I occupy in the bed, a wall that's defective but does indicate a limit, a wall that summons my bones triggering the historic pain in my spine, a pain in which I take refuge and which makes me wonder at the wounding and implacable build of bones, your bones. They hurt, they hurt, you say or you stop saying, and I'm glad your bones still hurt, that you feel them and that they make their presence felt every day or every night, each hour, in every minute, because you practically don't get out of bed, out of my bed, and you understand, you must, that you're only alive because of the power of your bones, those bones that boast of their pain, this so very solid mechanism that we have and we are bones, pure skeleton, don't you think? Don't start up with the business about the dress, just don't do it, don't go on, get your accounts out, give in to the accounts, leave the dress and the shop window, you say from your refuge in my wall.

You do it because it makes you sorry or afraid.

But this feeling is lighter, smaller than the one that recalls my capture a few months before yours. You fell after I did, briefly, you came out quickly and you're afraid, yes, you're afraid that when I'm sitting at the accounts, in front of the columns of numbers, I might remember, start to remember the effect of my fall. But we should not allow that, we cannot, the conditions that surrounded my coming out and how much and how they were going to pursue us, my capture. Not yours, mine. A fall that marked my body and exonerated my bones. My fall, not yours, no, never, because yours was the predictable fall of the embattled militant, surrounded by considerable infiltrations, just one more, but not me, not me. I was captured like a militant, like the militant who had been a part of several cells, a highly qualified linguist, a militant considered the most experienced in analysis and strategies, a cadre and yet, don't go on, please don't go on, you say to me. You have your back turned in bed, extended or extensive, comfortable, but no less in pain because you have been through a night that could be considered unbearable.

You talked during the night, you murmured during the night, you snored. You got up to go to the bathroom, you put on my slippers, you had three cups of tea, you smoked half a pack of cigarettes during the night, you had one nightmare at least, you tried to read the paper, you slunk off towards the bathroom to turn the pages in peace, you couldn't do it, the size of the letters betrayed you, you couldn't see, you couldn't read.

The letters defeated you.

You returned to the room. You took my arm in error believing it was your own. Let go of me, don't touch me, let me sleep, you blinked and then you pressed your eyelids with your fingers, yawning, you swallowed the piece of bread you'd put away under your pillow and when you thought it was a truly hellish night, you fell asleep, you did it without abandoning the sudden movements or the alternating space of murmuring and the odd vague complaint. (The cells crouched down, covering their ears.) You slept for a limited stretch of time. You shifted about in the bed, you woke me up or we woke up vaguely, defeated by a common sleep, a shared tiredness and alongside the need for that particular dress, the most primitive desire I can remember, I thought that with this dress, precisely because of its design, I needed to put on lipstick, and a violent, vermillion, glossy, provocative red became indispensable. A stellar red along with the highest heels I could find. A frantic search through the shop windows, through black pointed shoes, quite unsuitable footwear, shoes verging on the scandalous, with my too-red lips and the dress. Until the whole scale of the crisis appeared in the mirror that kept on reflecting a crazy, ferocious image, the belly, the belly, an image of me that terrorised us, do you remember?, do you remember?, and you didn't know what to do or what to say or where to escape to, while Ximena tried to pretend and even I wasn't sure myself, I wasn't sure about anything in front of this deadly reddened mirror that's showing an image out of a nightmare. No, I had chosen it, I had wandered pregnant by the shop window, I sought out the red, the most intense one, and I sought out the shoes, but the dress attacked me, it was the only spontaneous thing, that dress, mine, my sadness at the red and the shame of shoes that, no, did not go with it. We looked at ourselves in the mirror or through the mirror, I don't know. The three of us. Ximena, you and me. Now I look at the notebook, the rigidity of the columns, the order of the numbers, I measure how much we are worth, how much.

We spend little, we are worth little, I say to you.

Yes, yes, you answer me.

You say this with some relief. You prefer, I know, to go into the always uncomfortable subject of money rather than reviving the episode with the dress, its causes, its effects. You prefer anything, silence or a whole heap of words, you choose to go to the bathroom or the kitchen and you could even, I don't know, I'm not sure, go out onto the street, cross the pavement, walk with your most usual steps down a street that is becoming unrecognisable from one day to the next, small local grocers' shops, technological services, sales of spare parts. You'd prefer the most loathsome thing, the street, the one that reminds you how history goes on, continues on its course, seeps into the derelict paving-stones, into the new shop premises that stand there in the most fragile of hopes, the premises, the grocers', the services, the rapidly discontinued spare parts. You don't want to see or you cannot see and I, who understand you, understand you, so much so that I had to suspend our unnecessary walks, the day in the month when we agreed to take a stroll around the block and in a gesture that could only be sympathetic, I told you this, and registered your relief. Let's not go out, let's not, and I saw how you smiled, at me, with an old confidence.

Yes, you said to me, yes, why go out?

It's fine, I replied, there's no need, but you're going to walk around the room for about twenty minutes, you've got to walk, yes, yes. But you don't. You only go from the bed to the bathroom or the kitchen, you don't keep your side of the bargain, you don't deliver. Did you walk today?, I ask you as soon as I come into the room, did you do it? You didn't walk, you don't do it, you sleep at unearthly times and then who has to pay the price?, but you don't hear me because you're looking at the bag. Give me a bread roll, you say, and I'd like to deny you one because after all you don't deliver. You insist and then don't deliver, you don't deserve so much as a bit of bread. But I hand it over to you and you eat it trying not to let me see your fragile teeth on the dough or the crumbs you gather up and toss into your mouth and I know you have loose teeth, and two gone already. My teeth are loose too, all your teeth are coming out, aren't they? They're hurting you, yes, my molars, my gums, my teeth hurt, three molars and two teeth have broken but no, not a dentist, never. You have reconciled yourself. You have already surrendered to the ups and downs that biology assigns us, though perhaps we still expect too much from our bones. We trust that they will stay with us for as long as necessary, since what else have we got? Nothing, I say to you, we have nothing and we spend little, this month less than ever.

Less?, you say.

Yes, I answer, we have entered a low-cost phase, that's why I bought you cigarettes, the ones you liked, the ones you smoked before, remember? The ones I smoked before?, you say to me with noticeable vigour, yes.

Ah, yes, you say, the same ones from before.

You hesitate, you get muddled, you shrink in the bed, you demolish yourself. But what will they be like?, you say to me, what will they be like, those old cigarettes?, no, no, I can't, you say and toss the pack into the bin.

Dejected at my failure, I hand you another bread roll, one of those bread rolls that I know you so need and I know sustain us.

I had fallen already, trapped like a wild beast or a circus animal, right in the middle of the public highway, surrounded and captured. And later you would fall. A ruthless sum, the complete cell: all ten. Seven of us survived. Three dead. (The three dead are here, upright, ornamental, they sparkle in the darkness.) Before I had come out, you would fall. Four months of you neither alive nor dead. Finally we had to meet again. We did so ensnared in acute bewilderment. My condition obliged you to suspend your pain, your offence, the sum total of humiliations. The terror.

No, you said, no.

You looked at me and sitting there on the chair in the room I'd managed to get, this room, the same one, you took your head in your hands to hide, or to avoid the gravity of my appearance. You looked ravaged by a cataclysm. Yes, my inclement nature was speaking to you, back turned to any reason. But what could I do. What can I do?, I said to you. I didn't have, you understand, didn't have one single alternative. I was furious, yes, hurt, furious. Collapsed and furious, astonished and furious, terrified. Every feeling, each one belonged to me, they were mine and you showed up crushed after a time that no chronology could explain to add your sorrow to mine, your bitterness on top of my already impressive bitterness, a shock that sought to diminish my own. You showed up half alive or half dead, you returned armed with an impenetrable distance in the face of my misfortune.

'Things are the way they are.'

That's what I said when faced with your attempt at appropriation. I know I managed, out of some unsuspected place, some leftover strength and rage. I know too that I was about to shout or to cry but even so, my legitimate feelings aside, I'm sure that if you'd progressed even an inch in your accusations I would have killed you. Everything was occurring as if in a bad dream. But now I have to sleep or I have to die or I have to escape. But where?, where?, once the century has dislodged us. A hundred years already, and despite knowing that everything was completed in a distant past, in another century and, even more than this, in another millennium, a thousand years really, there it is, the whole recent century or the thousand years, outdated and treacherous years, that are laughing with a vile gesture flaunting the trail of misfortune they leave behind.

I know, I understand, of course I do. I know and I understand. Historical processes are emphasised or they fade away, they occur in a tension that can only be fleetingly diminished. I am or was a cadre. I did my training serenely but with utter decisiveness, I did it with an attitude marked by tenacity and ordered in lucidity and in a never naïve understanding of history. They were there, available for us or for me, the leading figures, old already, those figures who were cold but, no, not obsolete let alone mistaken.

Not that.

I devoured the aura of those figures who now, oh no, no, no, who now cannot be named. Frozen and lucid and still supreme in their mistakes, but which mistakes? Perhaps it is a mistake to state that: 'The conditions of bourgeois society are too narrow to comprise the wealth created by them. And how does the bourgeoisie get over these crises? On the one hand by enforced destruction of a mass of productive forces; on the other, by the conquest of new markets, and by the more thorough exploitation of the old ones. That is to say, by paving the way for more extensive and more destructive crises, and by diminishing the means whereby crises are prevented.' A self-absorbed lucidity, an irrefutable mise-en-scène, a trajectory that contains a thousand years, a hundred, of history. Yes, isn't that right?, but never, ever did I think about the autonomous functioning of the body, its cyclical surprise and its calamity. Never in your astonished or disgusted face, yours, in the hours of a tragic reunion, my tragic but fleeting survival. Three dead: crazy Jiménez, Pedro Cevallos and Luis or Lucho as we called him. (The three dead men walk their terrible contamination around the room. The attitude they adopt is cynical or ironic.)

Lucho, short, self-composed, solemn.

Lucho who would travel from Rancagua to arrive at the exact time, never late, not ever. At the precise time for the cell's meeting, a secret militant, much loved and serious, composed and solemn, who never ever, on any occasion, laughed out loud. Lucho who got impatient but hid his impatience about some comment or other that was outside the scope of the meeting. Nothing, nothing ever from outside. Because that's what he was like. He would not allow any rumour let alone any allusion to anything that could be considered personal. He hated that, that's something he hated, he refused questions, never shared an opinion that went beyond the cell's own issues. Lucho didn't laugh, or ask, and avoided any personal connection. That's what he was like. It's just what he was like. Rather short and dark and serious, so much so that he inspired a vague rejection or instilled a respect mixed with discomfort because he reminded us relentlessly that we were a cell, that was all, that between us there was nothing personal or, even worse, intimate, that we had no right to laugh or to kiss or to hate one another outside the frame of the cell. Lucho, the alias, who travelled from Rancagua, strict and sad, formal and sad, punctual and sad with his most legitimate face, a face that was not secret. Lucho didn't laugh and he took the bus back to Rancagua at the exact moment the meeting ended and he didn't have so much as a sip of coffee, just a glass of water.

Water for Lucho, just tap water.

The same Lucho who didn't want to, couldn't, did not accept his capture or the blows and each one of the planned scientific injuries and taking a historical decision, far removed from any kind of individualism, Lucho, with that mining-country frugality, his own Rancagua frugality that was covered up with the parsimony he cultivated, hanged himself like a militant. He planned it seriously and sadly, rigorously using whatever rags he had about him.

Crazy Jiménez and Pedro Cevallos, meanwhile, were brought down the same way countless other cell members were dying, from among those cells that fell and, among so many aliases, those two, Jiménez and Cevallos, weren't able to survive. A stroke of bad luck, you said, it's unlucky and understandable, part of the process, could have been me, anybody, forget about it, you said, you're tiring me, I'm getting tired, that's enough. We fell and died after the cell had already experienced its crisis and the break had occurred, when it was all over. But we fell as an active cell would have fallen, our organisms combined around one sole objective: the cell, the cell.

It's been a thousand years.

All of us already formed the anonymous surface of the dead cadres of another century, surrendered to the thousand years that pass in the newspapers we read, or that we stop reading, in the buses that take me and bring me back, in the stores, the shop premises, the ever fleeting or subtle offices you hate much, much, so very much more than I do. Don't tell me, I don't want to know, I'm not interested, did you bring my cigarettes?, did you bring me them?, you didn't? Yes, here they are. I hand you the packet of cigarettes, put another in the bag, the other that you will inevitably smoke, two packs I incorporate into the column of numbers that I will analyse this evening. I go to put on my glasses, the last ones I bought out on the street, and which were displayed strewn across the pavement. I bent down, I put them on, I looked at the signs to be sure that my calculations are correct and that they support our cell, a cell from another century or from another millennium, now determined to get hold of tea, rice, a reasonable amount of oil, a bag of sugar. A late-developing cell that remains in a larval state, seemingly deactivated, an appearance that is deceptive, because we know what we know: that, yes, we do have certain important skills, despite the bones, our bones, millennial ones, being pressured by disagreeable calcifications, or although the gaze that belongs to the optic nerve can't manage to constitute the pictures correctly, we are still a cell, we know that, deactivated and larval or almost blind, imperfect, but solid, isn't that so? Lucho, you say to me, was ultimately, in the most concrete sense, a reactionary, a clerical socialist. He sought protection in a histrionic act endowed with fake value, a bourgeois who acted in the guise of a Christian asceticism. That's what he was. You say it bluntly and in one respect, I know, your analysis is accurate; yet I challenge you and I raise my voice, upset; the improvised rope he put around his neck, that piece of fabric he managed to retrieve from an unbelievably hostile environment, cannot be reduced to simple histrionics or to a loathsomely religious factor. It was a piece of cell work, a materialist undertaking, thoroughly achieved, that led to the ultimate success. You, I say, are using overly simplistic thinking, leaving out parts of the elements, the most persuasive elements, the ones that lie behind simple appearances, behind any illusions.

We fall silent, we ponder.

While I put my hand on the wall, your ironic reference to a clerical socialism is prowling inside my head, aggravated by the insidious and equally ironic qualifier contained in your mention of an act clad in the echoes of a Christian asceticism. We toss and turn in bed weighing up the arguments. I understand, with extreme clarity, that you cannot sleep when faced with my clarification or precision around the materialist work with the rope or the fabric or the piece of trousers that made up part of his plan to achieve an ending. You don't sleep because I have constructed an argument that makes your analysis teeter, that punctures it and affects it. It's a struggle for us to sleep amid the difficulty of our bones that are also affected by the discomfort of calcifications, calcifications that exist and that we don't need tests to confirm. We're a cell, we are alert to ourselves like the cell we are. We can even diagnose ourselves. We don't need any technology nor to get ourselves to ultra-sophisticated medical imaging devices, those ones about which, no, you don't want to find out let alone understand in order to confirm that we have calcifications on our bones, that our bones are damaged and that your back hurts and your hip is afflicted by osteoarthritis and although we know we could access a latest-generation plastic hip or knee, microscopically crimped to almost imperceptible metal wires, we won't do it, we expect too much of our bones, we gamble on them, on the boniest history that should not be interfered with or intervened in and whose wasting is part of a materialistic process that it's necessary and, further, essential to deal with. We need to talk about Lucho, as we used to call him, we need to agree who he was exactly and which sphere his act related to, what he did in reality and how, from his act, we might understand his role in the cell we inhabited. To resume talking about Lucho, from the mining country, serious, short and extremely formal. Not stopping, each of us putting forward their argument, dismantling the arguments, aggravating them, pushing them to their limit, until we can plot a map of the situation and I manage to turn around your rejection of the suicide, your contempt for him. Your unshakeable perspective on the rope or the pieces of fabric or bits of trousers.

We're back to back on the bed, thinking.

But at our reunion, so many years ago, in the last century, here in this same room, in the abstract room that still survives in this century, we did not talk about Lucho then. We knew about his act, but the situation turned us in on ourselves, or on myself, to be more precise. You looked at me first astonished and then I'd say clearly uncomfortable and then hinting at a deep disgust. The nuances of the look in your eyes were successive and swift. I sat on the chair, you did the same on the one opposite, you rested your head in your hands, then, slowly, theatrically, you gradually withdrew your fingers. You tried, I know you tried, to find the words that were the most sensible and, up to a point, affectionate. However, you were not able to sustain them and the accusation came, the one that, of course, I was expecting, I expected it through the four months when you were neither alive nor dead or you were already dead as was I. I thought, over those four months, that you were going to say to me what you said to me because your reason wouldn't be able to hold out and you would surrender to the anarchic strength of your feelings.

But while I was right that you were going to say it, I didn't think about the choice or about the direction of your brutal, mean words: 'Why didn't you get rid of it'. An undeserved, coarse phrase that could only be understood as an insult. 'Things are as they are.' My heart was beating, my hands were shaking with anger, if you said one more destructive word, I was ready to kill you. Any old how. I got up from the chair to open the door and throw you, with no violence, out of the room. I wanted to do it and you noticed. I've got nowhere to go, you said, nowhere's safe, I can't go. Your words were simple and there was a humility patrolling around their tone.

Stay, I said to you, stay.

And that was how you came to walk over to the bed, stretched out, and complained, and fell asleep. You were tired. I climbed onto the corner of the bed, of my bed, and I settled into the patch that was still free. I realised, as you slept, that a new torment was beginning for me, and for us both, a contest for the space, a hitherto unknown way of living together avoiding the violence of the night. 'Why didn't you get rid of it,' you said in the midst of your rage and your disgust, but how, how was I supposed to have done that, I was a captured cell who was neither alive nor dead, a simple body that fell victim to too many countless injuries, assaulted in its biology, in mine. A biology that functioned, and that responded. When you woke, the light was still illuminating the room. You turned around and tried to put your hand on my head. A fake attempt, far too artificial, that I didn't dare to repel perhaps because I needed your hand on my head, and I also needed you to be there, right there, in spite of the wretchedness of the space and of the crying of the boy or the laughing of the boy or the indeterminate sounds of the boy or the silence of the boy who would later arrive and who forced you to sleep on the floor, on a blanket, next to us, because, no, all three of us did not fit onto the bed. You woke up, you put my hand on your head, a lying hand. Do you have any bread?, you asked me. Yes, I answered. But there was a decent and even poetic moment, a moment, just one, because when you got up and held out your arm to help me off the bed, you did it in a way that was kind and true. Yes, you were pierced through with a kindness that was completely real, and true.

On the day we met again, I went to the kitchen to prepare our cups of tea. While waiting for the kettle to boil I devoted my time to spreading the butter on the bread. I already had it planned: the tea, the butter, the bread, the tray. When I walked towards the kitchen, you said to me: 'I'll do it.' No, I answered, I can still manage. My words contained a hint of irony. A hint that was sparse but still ironic and, in spite of the crushing tension, you managed a smile. You set the two chairs, mine and yours, around the table. There were conflicting feelings between us, fluttering on top of the bread, steaming over the cups of tea, hovering around our faces. We felt, I know it, at one point, relieved and comforted because after months we were meeting again in the room, alive or you might say almost alive (dead, we were already dead). Protected by walls I had chosen. No, I hadn't chosen them, it was Ximena who'd done that, when she said to me: I've found you a place, but you don't have to go out, no, you don't go out for any reason, get it? Not just yet, not for now, you do it later, after the kid's born. I pass you the sugar, here you go, here's your spoon. While I talked to you about the sugar, I was thinking about how we were alive, how in spite of everything we still had our familiar faces that had known each other since the start of adolescence. We remained, in a way, alive (no, no), having a cup of tea, immersed in an ultimate adversity we never could have imagined. What are you going to do, you asked me. No, what you said to me was: what are we going to

119

do? Ximena, I answered you, she's going to take care of everything for as long as necessary, she's done it already, she comes and goes, handles things, although, of course, she's doing what she can, you know. Oh yes, Ximena. Each of us silent, pierced through with images that, even in their differences, contained us. We didn't know how to talk to each other or what to say, but we also understood that we ought to start, it was most pressing that we begin a process of organisation. We needed to organise and to present Ximena with a definitive plan, a coherent and precise blueprint. I, in those months, depended on a Ximena who came and went, seemingly obsessed, do eat, eat, as I tried to chew, to consume, to obey.

Eat, you've got to eat. Eat.

But hunger had withdrawn, though I did try, I did because she was so obsessed with food, with mine, it mattered to her, it was the only thing that mattered to her. Eat. And I had to do it, to eat, even though I wasn't hungry nor even knew what hunger was, because there was Ximena coming in and out of the room, at times that were never the same, at any time, the most surprising ones, rigorously following the basic template of the security measures we knew so well and which, nonetheless, failed, they failed and the one moment when her concern ceased was when the spoon was going into my mouth and she was checking how I swallowed, how the plate would be emptying and then, looking at the almost empty plate, I can't have any more, I can't, she breathed or sighed, satisfied that I'd eaten, I'd done it to tend to Ximena's purpose, I'm not hungry, I'm not hungry and yet the oppressiveness of her blather, eat, eat and when she left the room, militant self-denial fulfilled, the vomiting would begin or the disgust or the extreme feeling of a repulsive satiety, a really dirty feeling, a biological assault imposed in the face of a radical lack of hunger, and yet, without hunger, without any need, out of some mere common sense, understandable, basic but paradoxically inhuman, I had to eat, out of obligation, out of Ximena's self-imposed obligation, because you're going to die, you really are going to die, as if the word death had the slightest relevance to me.

Eat.

Eat. On those days without hunger, surrendered to the prolixity of Ximena who sought to avoid the compassion that did occasionally assail her, Ximena who fought to stay within a militant's conviction or hard graft, stripped of any emotions, surrendered to her political task of supporting the survivors, taking care of security, risking herself for the survivors, going out onto the street, Ximena, scared, her heart racing when confronted with cars that stopped abruptly or overly defined faces that looked at her or might look at her. Or solid bodies that were going to grab her from behind until her spine was in pieces or would get her into a car or would kill her with a single well-aimed shot to the head. Ximena, walking or getting off buses in pursuit of the survivors for them to go back to being who they were, to drop their baleful expressions or their misfortunes or their memories or their whims, eat, eat, gathering up pieces of decimated cells, fulfilling her task like this, an uncertain task carried out by clandestine cadres who were also falling and falling, eat, don't go out, don't turn the light on, hang in there, hang in there for a month or two, not long now, you've fewer and fewer months left.

We drank tea, sitting at the table.

Does Ximena seem trustworthy to you?, you asked me. I looked at you, amazed, what are you saying? You never know any more, you said, there are reversals, betrayals, planned handovers. Oh no, I said to you, not Ximena, not her. Are you sure? Yes, I'm sure, I'm convinced, I'm sure.

As I said it, a shadow of doubt, inevitable or unthinkable, assailed me. After all, who was Ximena, what cadre had she belonged to, how many cells had she been active in, what had her contributions been, where had her role come from. Ximena, the tall one. Her stature complicated her, enlivened her, gave her detail, but it was right there, her height and her militancy. I struggled to picture Ximena, tall and exact, a Ximena who'd been a part of the second cell we were a part of and who now seemed ready and willing, perhaps excessively steeped in a self-denial that at times confused us. But Ximena, beyond her gestures, responded and acted according to every pre-determined procedure. No, what you're insinuating, it's impossible. Nothing's impossible now, you know that, or you don't know it but believe me, the infiltrations, removals, pursuits, reversals, the successive captures, the ruptures, the doubt. I looked at you and saw how the expression in your eyes became inflamed to a critical point that disturbed me too much.

Shut up, I said.

I understood that my order, which might have been excessively violent, was necessary to dislodge your obsessions and focus us on ourselves. What are we going to do?, you said to me. Yes, I answered you, what are we going to do? It was getting dark. The room couldn't contain still less give form to an evening that appeared luminous and mild, promising a benign nature capable of producing a beauty it was impossible to ignore. Though I was in the room, sitting at the table, beyond the now empty tea cups, I knew that outside, on that exact evening, a clean and substantial solar spectacle was unfolding. I thought about the sea, I also thought uncontrollably about the fullness of the hills intensified by a falling light and I thought that you were there. And because you were there, sitting around the table, the mechanisms were going to be put in order and I could start to eat without distress because nature was stubbornly cyclical and we would need to understand it and, no, no, only to despise it. I wanted to tell you this, to talk to you about the sun and even the sea, despite having experienced your indifference towards nature, your evident disdain, like that afternoon we went to the beach together for the first time, taking advantage of the public holidays. It wasn't that those particular days, the holidays, were especially lovely ones, that wasn't it, what captivated me was the sight of the open space, of the evident dilemma of the horizon, the perception of a horizon cut through by the water which just transformed into a line and brought the always tense figure of the encounter to a geometrical resolution. We saw the sea, we looked at it with the naïve concentration typical of tourists. We sat on one of the benches on the esplanade and there we remained, still, silent. I thought we were sharing a moment that was unique and, in its way, decisive; but I soon had to give up.

Not you. Not you.

You were thinking about the next meeting, that's what you said to me while seated on one of the metal benches, you talked to me about your plan to get them to approve, and speedily, the agreements. You said this to me as we faced the sea, looking at the precise geometry of the line and the striking tidiness of the horizon. I understood that you were still at the centre of the cell, that you would remain there and that there could be no landscape or natural event that could separate you. You hadn't seen a thing, none of the outside space, the only images in operation were the ones unfolding inside your head.

I was shocked at your indifference or your incredible insensitivity. But at the same time, I felt it was mine, this sea that was capable of sketching a horizon. The sea belonged to me, and the magnitude of an unsuspected space. We were urban, that's what we were and although I understood that I was captivated by a nature I didn't inhabit or that didn't belong to me and that my emotion was, in a way, predictable and no doubt, fleeting or even worse than this could be considered banal, still I took possession. I answered you automatically, yes, yes, I said to you, but I continued to be absorbed by the swell, with my back to the cell and to your desire to get those agreements approved without any questioning. But while we drank our tea, in those hours of meeting each other again, I felt a similar impact. I was anticipating a sun that was avoiding occupying its power to the maximum, that possibility distracted me or separated me from the obligation of confronting the reality in which our lives were going to unfold. The setting sun also obliged me to cut myself off from Ximena and her dangerous proximity. And it obliged me especially to understand that I was tied to a nature, my own, that had finished tying up its signs.

Ximena will provide the logistical support, I said. What?, you asked, your tone astonished or scared. Yes, she's already getting ready, we agreed, the matter of the birth is already settled. You realised you had no choice. We couldn't show up at the hospital, we wouldn't do it because inside, in its hostile rooms, I would only find or we would only find the most concrete possibility of a certain death. I won't go to hospital, I said to you, you do understand, don't you? Yes, you answered. And then I dared to tell you about the whole plan, you're going to do it, I said to you, you'll do it yourself, but Ximena will give you the guidelines, the correct steps, she'll show you each of the necessary movements. And what's more, I said to you, she's writing up a manual for you to practise it, learn it, memorise and understand it, for you to feel confident.

No, no, I can't, you said. Not that.

You were deathly pale, about to collapse. Your refusal was vigorous and it was sincere, but useless. I thought about how I'd rushed, I thought I'd been clumsy in informing you of the plan, I thought too that my words contained a kind of revenge. After all you were returning from having weathered the most calamitous time your body could possibly experience, but the extreme nature of my situation removed you from yourself, you were returning to face my drama and, in the room, in the middle of the afternoon, our crushing decline was exposed. Well, well, this is one of the results of the historical era, the signs of the time, we knew that, I said. That's how it is, always, I insisted. We studied it or I did, I added. It's part of a programme that gets repeated over and over. In that way I sought to dilute the effect of the plan we had drawn up. I drew it up myself. I did it after pondering and assessing the options. But beyond the visions and fantasies that inevitably assailed me, never, ever could I have foreseen how the threshold of the pain and the blood would manifest itself. Your bloody hands, a surgeon's or a butcher's hands, your fierce face, your rage, the open decision that we would die, the boy and me, our savage deaths, your trembling mouth, the hatred of those long, stretched-out hours, waiting, waiting for the process to be over, both of us uncertain of its scale, and you terrified, despising me and despising yourself with no respite, maintaining that it was my fault, mine, and there, exactly there, that's where the contempt for yourself was rooted, your inability to leave, to give up on the cell into which we were going to be converted, to go out onto the street, agree on a new location, to renounce a union that had no foundations. To go out to find some shelter that would allow you to survive. You could do it, you could go off and look for Gómez who at the time was still helping out and fighting to retrieve and re-activate cells. (Gómez is sitting on the edge of our bed and he shows his broken arm like a trophy, the cells are furious at his individualism.)

You could get in touch with Gómez.

Explain to Gómez about the reasons for your flight, he'd understand, he'd support you, you were a living cadre who was urgently needed. Go to Gómez and say, no, I couldn't do it, no. Escape and, in the middle of some horrible pains and the fleeting effect of the ether, in the middle of my most implacable nature, faced with your unconcealable bitterness, I couldn't stop repeating angrily, viciously, hatefully, go, go to Gómez, he'll help you out, he'll definitely do it, Gómez is trustworthy, trustworthy, you can believe Gómez, he's totally immune to the infiltrations, the snitching, the planned handovers, and murmuring through sharp, gritted teeth, just go, you want to kill me, yes that's what you want, you're killing me, I'm dying, help me, give me more ether, hurry I'm going to die. But when you came back, the day of our reencounter, in this room, the very same room, we were still tending our recent wounds and so, when I said to you, you're going to do it, you answered without hesitation, with the certainty, the fearlessness and the bravery of the best and most disciplined militant, yes, I'll do it, I'll do it because we can't go to the hospital. I'll take care of it. And you added: give me Ximena's manual, let me have all the instructions at once.

Not eating at all?, I ask. Really, nothing all day? Why not?

Because she doesn't want to. That's why she's not eating.

We need to eat. We need to feed ourselves.

I say this as I bend over and pull back the sheets covering her. I start to unbutton her nightie. I look at what I know so well, her terminal absence; the grey colour that defines her, the stiff, twisted hands on top of the bedspread. The terrible bedsores destroying her. I also see the anxious, desperate look on the face of her sister, her only sister, seated on the chair in the room, watchful. The sister who awaits me and who fears me, who regrets no longer being able to wash her or sit her up in bed. The sister who projects herself into the disastrous body she watches over and feeds, surrendered to her understanding of the illness, captive to its symptoms and its signs.

Can I help?, she says to me.

No, I answer, there's no need.

She's miles away, indifferent, she says. She completely ignores me now.

She's very sick, I answer.

Yes, she says, that's true, but she's always been obstinate, stubborn.

I lay her across the bed, find the position that will allow me to remove her underwear, and her wet diaper, then I leave them in the basket beside the bed. I get the washbowl with warm water that is already waiting on the nightstand and I clean between her legs with a soft sponge.

Cover her up, her sister says to me, she's going to catch cold.

Wait just a little, I answer, I'll cover her up in a moment.

No, no, no, she says to me, cover her up right now. She's blue, can't you see she's turning blue?

But then I can't clean her.

No, don't clean her today, don't, just let her rest. Go on, go on home. But I'll pay you, here, here. Of course I'm going to pay you. Come back next week. Please, leave us alone.

Very well, I answer, fine, as you wish.

And nothing, nothing at all to do with the neighbours, you're to tilt your head and exchange a few words only if necessary, words that are neutral, wary, everyday. Ximena spoke without hesitating, she was talking from the very heart of the manual. And that is how I did it or we did it. We could live without the neighbours' curiosity, we avoided them. It wasn't difficult, we already had extensive experience, we knew how to make things vanish. We transformed into shadows or reduced the neighbours to shadows. You remember?, you remember? But it's late now. Everything has rushed ahead. We're no longer exactly alive (dead, yes, dead) after the hundred, the thousand years we had to endure. Exhausted, our bones dislocated, the faces we once had now ruined, you remember? Or maybe we never had them, maybe there never were faces, I don't know. But when I came out of my imprisonment, there was Ximena. When she saw me she was even careful with the direction, the exact shade, the pointedness of her gaze. She never allowed herself to show the least emotion at what I had coldly communicated to her. Rather she went out of her way to express her satisfaction because a militant was emerging partly alive, I was emerging onto the street and she was waiting to take me to the place she'd managed to get hold of, a space, a space. A safe place, she said.

Yes, I answered her. Thank you, I said.

Thank you, I murmured amid a crushing absence. I said it to her because I had, after all, been trained in politeness, I said it just because, out of habit. Thank you, and as I spoke each of the sounds, I hated the words, I had withdrawn from those words, I knew there was nothing, absolutely nothing I had to thank her for, on the contrary, the nightmare was the sign, I myself was the living proof of a total disorder, the unleashing of evil, the effect of a terrible result or a joke or a frighteningly melodramatic bit of proof. When I knew that the boy was coming, I could have laughed or cried or I could have taken refuge in a predictable self-pity. I didn't. But I remember that I positioned myself in a feeling of sharp contempt. Although behind the contempt, a remnant or a piece of me knew that I was going to hold out because the boy, my own, was irreversible and innocent or he was nothing. Nothing but a boy who could not be blamed. Or who could be blamed though it was unnecessary now.

I was an analyst.

I was an analyst. I was ready to weigh up each and every condition and the boy in me. The captivity, the boy and me. A beautiful or glorious boy, who was already walking and beginning to express his first words, some minimal, narrow words, my boy, who after two years, between some powerful death rattles wasn't, no, he was not going to survive. I can't say anything, I shouldn't. After a century I watch you now asleep or awake, thinking with no horizon, stretched out on the bed. The bed and you, that's the agreement, the sheets and my pillow, the whole century, the thousand collapsed years. There you remain, in the room, curled up, with your cranium (your skull) between the pillow and the sheet, lying there, while I go out and walk unhesitatingly along the straight line of the pavement, I arrive at the bus-stop and, when the time comes, I briskly climb aboard the local bus, ordinary, mass-produced, crammed into a bus that must complete its lengthy route to which I have to submit in order to arrive promptly at the house, at the job, at the woman and each of her infinite details.

Beside my window the sirens howl. I understand that, further off, in the next neighbourhood, a shooting has occurred, a bank robbery. One of the bullets was a direct hit on the security guard, a man of about thirty, in his blue uniform, dark-skinned, but, no, not slim. A guard who prior to the gunshot had a presence. Yes, he'd had a presence because he was a diligent, silent, armed man. But now the guard falls to the floor, on his side, foetal, curled up, fatally wounded. Death, his own, lodged in the misery of one of his lungs and through the hole, due to the precision of the shot, through the irreversible severity of the wound, the blood rushes, a blood that is common and current, though hindered by the insistent clots that ruin the most watery elegance that has always characterised this red. Amid a minor or almost derisory or anodyne agony the guard is dying and the woman dies too, killed by her stupid hunger for the limelight. She dies irreversibly, strewn slowly across the floor, she's dying from two, three well-aimed shots to the head. She dies and she dies as though she were the only creature in the entire universe.

She dies inwardly, confused.

She agonises, convulsing.

Stretched out like that on the ground, she jerks about, because the bullets in her head compel her to these absurd, uncontrolled movements, and there, the encephalic mass, a significant part of her brains, slide over the floor of the bank, soiling its neat tiles. They are soiled and degraded by this thick, impure matter that drains out of the agonised head of the woman who is dying and dying in a savage act that does not horrify but rather provokes nausea. The public spectacle of this woman of, how old?, around forty, forty-five, what does it matter, a uniformed executive, nervous when faced with a robbery, who didn't know how to or couldn't withdraw or didn't want to keep out of what was happening let alone do without screaming and didn't forgo insults either, and didn't, she just didn't, hide her haughty contempt for the robbers, until the two or three bullets brought her down, her eyes rolled upwards, the convulsions, legs mobile and final, the ludicrousness of a body governed by its own neurology, the surprising workings of the body. The woman dies more quickly or more noisily than the guard, they both die pervaded by different signs. The guard more modest, more committed or circumspect or absent in the minutes of his death, so different from the convulsive woman, with abstract neurons scattered on a floor that could no longer be considered pristine.

Oh, how these oppressive sirens scare us.

The ambulances seem to be connected to the speeding cars of the police. All the bodies: the doctors and the repressive silhouettes of a frigid state police, tread in the organic matter, ruin the death rattles of the brainless woman and don't pause at this abject contaminated ground, no, they don't, and nor do they feel sorry for the guard who still hasn't finished dying, who is clinging to himself, although he's already dead, he is, so the doctor will declare him with all his vast meticulous indifference. Both of them pallid, astonishingly pale, animated only by the noticeable trails of blood adorning them. And oh, the bank invaded by the police and the medical teams and the encephalic mass of the woman and the active urgency of the teams that move, spurred on or vigorous, faced with a blood that excites them, and validates them.

The sirens, the sirens cut through and into the passing of the traffic, providing the city with the yelling it needs, while, further on, two blocks or five, it could be five, the recurrent and inevitable young man will straight away, without hesitating, without the least glimmer of weakness, with astonishing precision, shatter the car's windscreen. He will do it with all the power of his musculature transferred into the stone, a stone he is holding with the vigour that his deep-seated resentment bestows on him. The stone with which he is going to injure the man with no great fuss. He will knock the car's driver sideways, a guy who was noticeably overweight, fifty years old, an engineer. An industrial engineer who's going to end up with his face in an impossible condition, his jawbone broken, his eye damaged, damaged, a professional man (an engineer) who cannot seem to understand the stone at all, the hand that attacked the glass or even the onslaught of the young man's body. He won't understand it due to the acute haste in which he found himself surrounded. The industrial engineer, the fifty-year-old male, now lies halfway between lucidity and unconsciousness, subjected to blood, a blood that appals him, wakes him and, simultaneously, puts him to sleep, while with all the momentum of his arm, the young man opens the car door, quickly, quickly to search the pockets of the man who's bleeding, takes out his wallet (the money, his chequebook, the engineer's cards, his stereotypical family photos, how very common those photos are), but the attack, despite being so fleeting, has already been noticed. The pedestrians see him, and the motorists, and they fear him.

They fear him and do not act.

A dramatic silence passes over the block, nobody goes to help or intervenes. They keep away. The man injured by the stone covers his face with his hands. I'm going to die. I'm going to die and he surrenders to the pain. The young man disappears in a perfect and effective sprint. The first motorist appears. His presence coincides with that of the pedestrian and both remain engrossed, looking at the driver slumped on the seat, entirely captive to the image of the man with the broken jawbone. The bones of his face will undergo hurried emergency surgery but he is never going to recover, never the face he had before, it won't be possible. Just like you, just like you. Your cheekbone fractured, they struck you in the face with an iron bar, the metal left a noticeable mark on you. I didn't want to talk to you about your face, I didn't do it on the day we met again. The moment you arrived, I knew they'd broken your left cheekbone because you had a dent that wasn't dramatic, no, more dignified though very much there. Why am I thinking about your cheekbone. I open the handbag and I take out the cap that protects me from the water, it's faulty. I ought to buy a new one, how long do they last?, two or three months at most. A cap every three months, a plastic smock every month. The bus, its swaying seems to underline your cheekbone again, a dent that was there and that I didn't want to comment on. We didn't do it. We said nothing about your face, we didn't go into detail. That's how it was, that's how it had to be because any question, any account would have transported us to a territory we needed to avoid. I decided you had the same face as always, that there wasn't the least difference, that your features were constant.

I erased your face.

But I noticed at once that you had a new asymmetry to it, but you weren't able to do the same, you couldn't maintain the firmness of your stare let alone hold back the reproachful words: 'Why didn't you get rid of it'. Further off, amid the movements of the bus, I can make out the shop windows. And another, and another, lying idle, faintly dismantled, somehow neglected these shop windows and, behind the windows a series of sounds that could only be attributed to bullets, sharp and recognisable, bullets passing far in the distance but so, so many of them. They're robbing almost all the banks, the shopping centres exploding without let-up, their merchandise scattered across the mass-produced aisles, they're emptying the safes, security guards and police officers and customers die, one of the robbers dies, a little boy dies. They are stoning hundreds or thousands of cars, pilfering wallets, a man gets hysterical, he shouts and shouts driving one of the city blocks crazy, he shouts, howls, while in the luxury houses a terror is unleashed that is not altogether blameless.

They ransack, and ransack, and ransack.

The streets pass one by one, the stops one by one, the bullets, the young men and their stones, the impassive and transparent bank branches. Everyone is moving at an impassioned rhythm. But that's what the city's like, isn't it? Wild and feverish. Lively and rowdy, quite a spectacle.

But everything has normalised now. It looks, for a moment, like a city from another century or another millennium, mute and opaque. But at the street right opposite the bus route, in a remote house that some might even consider peripheral, the pregnant woman cannot withstand the first blow to her head and falls to the kitchen floor. The blow to her head dizzies her: its force and the dry, bony sound. She understands that she ought to get up, get up onto her two feet and try to run away, do it right now, stand up, but at the same time she knows the blow will fall again and again, chaotically on her body, her head, her ribs, her leg, a foot and her arm.

It broke both her hands.

This time she really is going to be killed, a crime of passion, another one, my own, on this exact day and when no more than seven minutes have gone by she will be lifeless on the kitchen floor. She knows it. She can tell she has minutes of life because the blow to her head, or to put it more accurately, the blows to her head were truly deadly. She is going to die in a certain way, the evening news will report her connection to a machine that will not revive her, it will only be there to shore up her ending, her dead brain. Out of partial modesty or censorship, the news will show only the tiniest part of the injuries, they will not show her head, and her blood-soaked hair, hair that's sticky. The last thing, truly the last thing the woman managed to think (perhaps it was no more than a word) was a command, stop, stop. Then nothing. Everything ceased meaning, it was gone. Her face that wasn't disfigured, not that, but very altered and swollen, historic. Like your cheek, the fractured cheekbone. Or like me. A bone that could be reconstructed until what was left behind was an indentation that marked your absence for ever. You arrived with your ill-treated bone, you came in, and sat down on the chair. After months. I sat down, too. The table, the same one we have now, stretched between us. Then you lay down on my bed and fell asleep. Now, as gunshots echo across the city, you will be sunk into the bed, the usual one, just as I get off the bus, as I walk as upright as I can, as I pretend that, no, no, my back doesn't hurt or my right knee, nor does my shoulder while I attempt on a perfectly ordinary walk to look like I'm somebody I know, someone I control. But I have doubts. I have doubts and I waver, astonished at the very possibility of being a woman I know and control.

The bus crawls forward. I turn with bureaucratic resignation towards the window. Through the glass the only thing that stands out is a grey landscape into which cold bodies intrude, walking at a predictable, human speed. Everything is in order or giving the appearance of a meticulous order. But now I look at the driver. I watch as he fulfils his role, which he does with a practised patience. I see his back or glimpse his profile. I notice his hands and their dextrous relationship to the metal. I am just another passenger, a victim of the delay, a mere urban cog. I did manage to get a seat and this allows me a bit of control over a limited area. The other passengers are transformed, under the position of my gaze, into mere fragments, pieces of backs, heads, a sudden profile, the haste of a hand on metal at the sight of the stop. We are few, and very similar to one another. Anonymous citizens captured in a locomotion that is obstructed by packed traffic that keeps us tense in our seats, waiting for the red of the traffic-lights to cease and the other bus to advance, the one in front of us. We are almost at a standstill or moving at a speed that's frankly exasperating while I cannot decide whether to look out of the window or pause on the driver and the pieces of the passengers. I look inside and outside. I'm distracted by the street and I'm distracted by the aisle. In reality, beyond my own desires, I can't move my gaze away from the street or from the inside of the bus, in regular succession: the street, the inside, as if I were a look-out or an informer compelled to take down a report.

The street, which is over-populated (we are, after all, travelling along a major road on the city's neural pathways), pushes me to look at the façades or the gardens or the trees or the series of bodies that walk at a speed not much different from the bus that is making no headway because it's blocked by another one that, in turn, though we can't be sure about this, has found itself trapped at a broken-down traffic-light or by an accident or someone being run over or a robbery or some indefinable traffic disturbance.

I could get off.

At the next stop.

Get off and walk the, how many, maybe twenty blocks separating me from the house. No, fifteen blocks. Maybe six stops, yes, six, plus the two blocks that I must of necessity cover on Wednesdays and after recognising the house, after stopping outside the railings, go through, press the doorbell, a doorbell that's sometimes out of order, after experiencing the tense wait until the door is opened for me, till it's opened for me by the skinny woman who's worked, they told me, in the house for ten years, knowing full well that she takes her time, that she hates opening the door, that after hearing the doorbell she walks down the hallway of the house, draws back the curtain and looks out the window to check who's coming, who's outside, she does this before peering out the door and when she recognises me, with a condescending attitude, she invites me into the house, the house on Wednesday morning, as her son said, clear and vigorous, not too early, at a time that's convenient, not first thing and much less in the afternoon, she sleeps till ten and in the afternoon she hasn't the strength or the spirits, mid-morning, that's the best time for her, more than that, it's really the only time that's possible and I absolutely cannot stress this enough, you'll have to arrive here at eleven or twelve latest, you understand? Press the bell that's sometimes out of order, I couldn't hear it, if I don't open up just give me a shout, because they still haven't fixed it, we haven't found somebody who can solve our problem with the doorbell, and wait for the skinny woman of indeterminate age, forty, though if you look closely, no more than thirty-five, opening the door with a mistrust that makes her glance left and right, scared of the street or suffering from a cold, coughing, what can I take?, my throat hurts, aren't you a nurse?, oh, so you aren't a nurse, and I was so sure you were a nurse, but all the same, what would you suggest for this cold?, while making no effort to hide the fact she's checking her watch, that's her job, keeping a check on my timing, my possible lateness or a disrespectful haste. As you're well aware, madam's son, who's in charge in this house, who keeps tabs on it, who stocks it up, who keeps track of the expenditure, who often gets annoyed at the prices, madam's son, he said eleven to you, between eleven and twelve, but madam's not too bad today, not too bad, you'll see her, just as well you're here now, because I can't get her up, she could fall, she could fall and what am I supposed to do then, oh no, no.

Walk those two blocks I know so well.

Get off at the right stop and then walk the two blocks, stop at the door and hope the doorbell does work this time so I can get into the house quickly and dodge the words of the skinny woman who's thirty-five years old, one metre seventy, about fifty kilos, with a dark mole on her cheek. Thin lips and a narrow forehead, and covered in a blue checked apron, always the same one, always clean. Black hair, slightly curly, her hands stripped of any rings, dark coffee-coloured eyes, short nails, thin hands, grey flats on her feet, sheer tights wrapped around her thin legs, tan-skinned, pale. Listen as her footsteps approach the door, as she opens the door to the house and then see the dark woman, peering out the doorway, with her blue checked apron, white checks, a standard, traditional uniform. Confirm her fear of the bell, of the street, a fear inscribed in her nervous or mistrustful expression, come in, come in, a dark woman of thirty-five, come in, as she looks at her watch and checks, like every Wednesday, that I have arrived on time, correctly occupying each one of the minutes available to me.

I know that when the traffic's back to normal I'm going to focus on counting the stops. I'll do it because it's a method I use to help me bear the days when I am obliged to travel the city. But today is Wednesday and the bus is moving at a pathetic speed, weighed down by the wreckage of a crash that's happened two stops ahead and which they're only just starting to clear. Two dead and one injured in this morning accident. But soon they will have removed the bodies and the injured person will be taken away, a young man, amidst a hellish howl of sirens to get him into the most critical area of the hospital. The site of the accident, as attested to by the curiosity of the citizenry, the presence of an investigating judge and his assistants, the firemen, the police, the ambulances who will leave a trail of noise along the whole exten-sive perimeter of their hysterical, theatrical journey, the enormous echoing of the ambulances, the squad cars and the fire engines, raising the alarm. And the police acting with their habitual distance to demonstrate the profes-sionalism they require.

Well-trained.

Canine.

I will arrive before the time is up, I'll arrive when there are minutes to spare before twelve o'clock and the door will be opened to me by the skinny woman who has worked faithfully for ten years in the same house and who renews, all through the ten years, the checked apron, white and blue, it's a dark blue, navy. She'll open the door to me with her usual expression, scared and mistrustful, her flat shoes and colourless tights and neat wavy hair framing her thin lips and the mole she has on her cheek. She'll look at the time on her small watch, with its round face, the faded numbers and the worn black leather strap around her wrist. She will do this automatically; the look and the watch, giving no indication of any offence, she'll look at the time while she tells me that madam, as she refers to the old woman, is doing well, that, though she's sleeping badly, she always does, she's still alive and is waiting for me, no, it's not that she's waiting for me, she urgently needs a thorough washing because she reeks, she smells and every accumulation of the smell infects the house more, and still more, the smell bothers her, as she's the one who has to put up with the smell and only I can get rid of it for a few hours, just for a few hours, because tomorrow Thursday the house will be the same again, infiltrated by a trailing stench that it becomes ever harder to live with.

If the bus gets back up to its proper speed, I'll arrive comfortably at a pleasant and appropriate time. If they're quick about getting the dead bodies out from inside the pulverised cars, if they shut their enormous or terrified eyes and after hastily rearranging their fractures or mutilations, one dead person, one of them, the book-keeper at a firm, didn't just end up with his head smashed but also experienced the mutilation of one of his legs, his leg cut off by the impact and the ferocious power of smashed metal. If they wrap them in the habitual black bags, if they cover them in the black plastic to protect them from the hungry eyes watching with no respite nor modesty because they want to look at them from up close, even closer, really right on top of the dead, millimetres away from their lifeless bodies, want to touch the dead, stand right in the blood, drag some of that blood on their shoes, and more than this, some of them lean in to exercise their daring or their right to put their hand on the ground till they're soaked with the blood that's draining along the street, while the firemen leave and the stretcher-bearers stay behind, aided by the doctors and, under the severe gaze of the police officers and the sullen gestures with which they disperse the curious bystanders, lift the injured man onto the stretcher, into the ambulance, hook him up to a critical saline drip, take his measurements, sound his chest for his biological functions and then, if the work of the judge who's taking the official minutes to record the dead is completed, only at that moment is it possible to disperse the eagerness of the group of curious bystanders who are preventing the resumption of the correct speed of the traffic.

I could arrive at the house after walking the two blocks, two blocks that aren't especially long, on a grey, cold day, walking with faster steps than usual so as to comply with the flimsy contract I established with the aim of ridding the house of an unbearable smell, as the woman who opens the door says every week, after looking out of the window to confirm who it is who's ringing the bell or if it's broken as has happened more than once, after drawing back the curtain, alerted by my banging on the wood, my hand hurts, knuckles red from so much knocking with them so that she'll open the door and she'll manage just for a day to remove the smell that is expanding progressively into each of the rooms, a smell that seeps through all the cracks and inhibits any enjoyment of food because the kitchen is unbreathable and she can't, no, no, I couldn't possibly clean madam myself, it's a job for a nurse like you, like you, though you're not a nurse, but that doesn't matter, it's not impor-tant you aren't a nurse, you just come here after walking

142

the two blocks to dislodge for one day, one day when the house is normalised, the smell, drive the smell away, bathe her, bathe madam, as she calls her, that lady who I don't know why or how she stays alive or maybe she stays alive only because she's lost her sight and her sense of smell, but not me, not me.

The firemen still haven't been able to free the dead bodies trapped in the cars' twisted metal. The two dead bodies. The man who's seriously or critically injured is breathing lightly sunk into his unconsciousness. The judge and his assistants have already shown up, as have the ambulances with the doctors and paramedics. The firemen and their impressive trucks, the police have leapt out of their cars, and together with the firemen are struggling to get the dead out from inside the vehicles. They'll manage it any minute now and when they lay them out on the pavement and the ground is covered in the blood of the dead and the hands and uniforms of the police turn red, stained, gorged on blood, after the doctors have certified the correct deaths, when they reunite the mutilated leg with the body of the incomplete dead man, certify their stopped hearts, devoid of the least trace of breathing, as soon as they get the ambulance to blare away with the injured man inside, only then will this bus resume its speed, no more than forty kilometres an hour, or rather thirty kilometres an hour, because that's just the right speed to jam up the city, to achieve a city that's truly modern and dysfunctional, not more than thirty in reality, to thereby demonstrate the success of a city that seeks to be a part of a consistent history. If we pick up speed to thirty kilometres an hour I will be able to get off at the stop that is two blocks from the house and I'll be able to walk quickly but assuredly for the five minutes or four, it'll take me, four, four minutes, not a minute longer, to arrive with a punctuality that inspires all the confidence in the world, a punctuality that allows the skinny woman to open the door to me with a smile on her lips because I'm not cheating her and I'm offering her the prospect, for which she is openly desperate, of a period of time, some hours, twenty-four with any luck, of relieving the house of the smell that's driving her crazy and keeping her permanently nauseated.

Go into the neglected or uncomfortable house, to the bedroom of madam, as the skinny woman calls her, and into the centre of a truly appalling smell. I'm inside. I take off the sheets, position madam, as she calls her, on the mattress, cover her up with a blanket, while I soak the sheets in the bathtub, sheets that are indescribable and I use my hand to detach a week's shit, a week of shit that gradually hardens to form a crust, which is sort of innocent, mixed with the urine, I don't know how this lady doesn't catch cold or die, being wet all week long, and what can I do, I'm not prepared for this, it's not what I was hired for, I haven't got the strength because she's heavy, she's heavy, you understand?, not me, I can't do it while I use my hand to detach the crusts of excrement, I detach them with my fingers because there's no longer any other way to do it and afterwards, with difficulty because of the weight of the sheets that are streaming water copiously, I hoick them up into the washing machine with all the strength I have and then I take off my plastic gloves, the thickest I could find, the gloves I use every Wednesday and which I always put on as soon as I come into the house, those gloves I had to buy specially for the sheets, so I can remove the crusts of excrement from them and then toss them into the machine. And I set the machine going, I hear its noise, I let its noise continue on its course while I go back into the bedroom and uncover madam, as she calls her, and who, I don't know, I can't tell if she's asleep or awake, no one could know for sure, and even though she's got her eyes open, she could be not seeing anything, not recognising anyone or making out any shapes she can't see, can't recognise, she can't completely sleep, nor is she awake, nor does she know when the shit comes out of her sphincter, still less the moments when she soaks herself through with the undeniable strength of the volume of urine that she is obliged to expel.

I approach the old lady and, supplied with each of the materials I have bought, the most effective for getting her cleaned on top of the bed, on that mattress stained by years of dirt, by the overlaying of substances and liquids, a mattress that might seem unbelievable or indestructible, a good mattress that withstands over and over the onslaught of the lady's body and which can bear the dry soap I use to relieve her skin, the skin that's on a body that doesn't express itself at all when I turn her around, nor when I move her head to unstick the hair that's damp with urine and put on the shampoo that doesn't need water and she doesn't register any bother when I put the useless diaper over her crotch and, in an absence that surprises me, her face with its open empty eyes, she doesn't flinch when I rub the cream onto her face, first the cleaning one because her face is a wreck, her face is dirty, and then I prepare it for the other cream, the next one, the one that will grant a transitory, fleeting moisture to a face already lacking a beginning and an end. And I look for the nightie in the drawer, I rummage, dig around in the lady's items of clothing until I find the nightie and I put it on her and do up the buttons one by one and then get ready for the hardest stage, arranging the clean sheets with the lady still on the mattress, performing a real miracle all on my own because I mustn't strain myself, I had made a commitment solely to the son who keeps this house, who pays my wage religiously, who complains about everything, who says the costs need to be brought down, I swore to that son I'd give her her food twice a day, some baby-food I pulp in the machine, it's a special, very quick one, because madam doesn't have any strength in her jaw and hardly opens her mouth and, in the middle of this smell you know already, I've got to give her that baby-food of hers twice a day, at one and at six, I've got to do it in spite of the retching or actually the vomit because if I don't do it this lady's going to starve to death on us.

I manage to put the clean sheets evenly on the bed. It's turned out well, very well made, the bed. And though my arms hurt, and my elbow, one of my shoulders, I take pleasure in my impeccable work and I'm grateful, in part, for the abyssal absence of the lady who puts up no resistance at all and to round off this Wednesday, I sprinkle a few drops of cheap cologne on the bed, a cologne bought at a nearby chemist's, the thriftiest that the skinny woman could find, a cologne that covers two or three days, because she, the skinny woman, on Thursday, Friday and maybe Saturday, tips too much of it onto the bed or onto the bedroom floor, with no thought to the expense, on top of the bed, desperate to hide the smell that lives here like a chronically dependent relative. I rinse the gloves, soak them with the detergent, rub them dry with the towel. Despite the protection the gloves offer me, I wash my hands with the bit of soap I find, I wash and wash my hands maniacally and after drying them, I put on my watch, the one with a metal strap and see to my satisfaction that I haven't taken more than an hour, sixty complete minutes to deal with what one might consider a difficult undertaking and when I emerge into the hallway, the skinny woman, covered in her checked apron and her colourless tights, hands me the envelope as she murmurs a sequence of phrases I refuse to hear and, before going out onto the street, I fold the envelope and put it carefully away at the bottom of my handbag. Still sitting inside a slow bus, which doesn't move, doesn't move, hoping to arrive on time. A specific time that should only ever be desperately precise. Still.

On this bed, on this same mattress, of course, if we can still call it that, the mattress: you, me and the ether. The ether was there to make it possible to withstand the inhuman moments. It was Ximena, Ximena who managed to get hold of it, a bottle, she said, a small bottle of ether, she said and she said: yes, I know, ether's not what it used to be, it ends up being laughable and even dangerous, but no, not dangerous, I don't think so, but what are we going to do, what are we going to do, we administer it, that was what she wrote, in slow, precise doses. You bring the sponge with the ether close to your nose, you inhale it like an addict and you'll be away, or you'll sleep or faint for a few moments, just a bit, OK? It won't be enough but it'll help, it will do that. Then she looked at you and said: you open the bottle, you soak the sponge with a few drops of ether and hand it over. She's got to hold it to her nose herself because you'll be down below, right?, working, getting the child out, taking out its head, gently, understand? After all it's a primitive process, common, it's an almost inconsequential event, hands rotating the head, the neck, the shoulders of the baby and we've got the ether. You resort to the ether only when the pain is killing her. Just a few drops in those moments the head is appearing, just at the instant when the shoulders are rushing out, when you think she might scream, I'm talking about real yelling, you understand? Only at that moment, while she's fainting or sinking from pain that you feel is real and concrete, a few drops of ether. Everything perfectly typed, never handwritten, never.

You were reading the memo carefully. It turned into your memo. What were you thinking? There's no longer any point in trying to guess or it's not that there's no point because I know, I know and Ximena knows that the two of you had another plan, a non-memo, a secret word connected to an emergency telephone. You had planned it. It was necessary and it was fair. Yes, an emergency plan to dispose of the dead, the little boy and me, if we died.

You did have it, yes, that plan.

I want you to get up right now, to get out of bed and for us to sit at the table, I need you to look me straight in the eye and tell me how our deaths would have worked, where our bodies would end up, who was involved as helpers, where we were going to disappear. We could have died, I say to you, the boy and me. But I don't say it, I just think I say it. I go carefully over the scenes, I try to put them in order so I can examine them, but they move too fast, they get muddled. Two centuries or more. Years on end or years upon years that coalesce to shape the commonest outlines of the skull. How could pain be evoked, the confused amazement of pain, with what images would it be possible to remake the rise of a violence that was concrete but, at the same time, was blurring into a striking abstraction. We were there, us two, absorbed in a childbirth that, no, did not surprise us.

This is how it was:

A cold process began, the same process Ximena had foretold. A process covered by the distance that housed a certain amount of pretence. There began, with no great fuss, an indeterminate physical discomfort.

I said to you:

Something's happening, or something's happening to me. Something organic, automatic, that's what it seemed like, alien. I was starting to receive the planned effects of an attack I could not repel. Everything I was feeling or that I could feel was related to a body that seemed strange to me and detached. We were going to die, the boy and me. We weren't prepared, we weren't, the cell failed. It wasn't able to foretell.

Isn't that true, Ximena?

Yes, it's true, she answers me, it's true, but make no mistake, we did foretell. We foretold the deaths, we did. But what does it matter, nothing exists any more, not one cell, they died.

(The cells, so disciplined, agree as they parade unremarkably around the room, they parade past to enact a habit: their completely round circuits.)

Have all the cells died, Ximena?

Yes, she answers me, all of them.

Who's the person you're talking to?, Who are the people you're talking to?, you say to me in an unusual voice. A voice that's odd, mysterious because you've got your head buried in the pillow, in our pillow, in the only one we have.

Let me sleep, you say.

But you don't sleep, it's a clumsy attempt to silence Ximena and me. You want peace, silence. You would say that you deserve both, peace and silence, you think they're what's right for you after you handed your bones and blood over to a century that plundered you, a century in which we naively believed and which hurled us down headlong towards a ridiculous hope. The century suffers. It still talks or murmurs, left, right and centre. It drags its dismal childish chains, it laughs at itself with loud guffaws that are harsh and pathetic. I hear it and it haunts me.

We died in the middle of an appalling labour.

I didn't manage to give birth to the coming century. The boy, my own, was born dead after my death. A sterile birth.

It was completely useless, Ximena.

I say this to her with total conviction.

Yes, I agree. It all turned out to be so useless, she answers.

Who are you talking to?, who are you talking to? I'm talking to Ximena, to her. We're talking about the deaths, the boy's death and mine. You gave me, I know, a huge amount of ether, that's how you killed us, with the ether. That was your task, your mission, that was the order from the last cell particle remaining. We needed to die. Yes, exactly. I was or we were going to die because that's what you and Ximena had decided, isn't that true? You reached the agreement after analysing a considerable number of factors, you wanted to protect yourselves and protect the atoms of cells that still had the potential to keep going. I know there was nothing personal in that decision, it was a security measure, simple but urgent.

No, no, you say to me, it wasn't like that.

Well, what happened, then?

When?, you say. And I think you're tired, tired of the night, of the small noises that seep through the walls, incomprehensible sounds that come from outside, from a city that to you is already quite unknown. You're tired.

I am, you say to me, tired.

You're dead, I answer you.

The bed and the ether, the blood and the ether, my legs and the ether, I don't know. I can't be sure about anything. The boy was born dead or died aged two.

Or he wasn't born. Or he wasn't born.

Time folds back into its own time. Who'd have thought it: now we have all the time in the world. That is literal, we had it just after time ended for us. It's confused and it's appalling. It's inexplicable. It is not material, let alone dialectic: it is a damned hieroglyphic. Ximena, you say to me, was the first, she got swallowed up by the time that she had left.

You want to lie. Ximena fell one morning, she was taken by surprise, they threatened her and carried her off. No, Ximena says to me, no, that's not how it was, it didn't even involve anyone surprising me, they followed me, I just didn't or couldn't find a place to shelter and I practically handed myself over, in a state of ecstasy or of delight as it meant putting an end to those days, the boy and you would be over, and the coming and going, the irregular pulsing of the cells. I died, that's true, says Ximena, convinced that he was going to kill you. He was going to kill you anyway, no, don't tell me you didn't know. A killer militant, a killer who was not remanded to any court, a crime nobody noticed, a death unpunished, he killed you and took advantage of his clandestine nature, of his dying militancy. But I knew it before my death, I read it in his head, because never did a single cell ever manage to win my total commitment. I had to be suspicious. He was going to make you pay for the business with the boy. She stays quiet, in silence because your movement in the bed demonstrates an open sign of reproach.

Ximena curls up into a ball. Sometimes it's hard for us to understand this bed, its infuriating difficulty.

We rest side by side on the bed, the three of us. I can just about put up with Ximena lying with us or between us, while you, meanwhile, are indifferent and permissive, you'd allow every single cell to take over our bed. Ximena thinks she ought to get up and go out, she's still fighting to find a millimetre of active cell. You, meanwhile, have nothing, no cause, just a body that compels you, your own, your body and your arthritis and the wavering of your liver or the acidic grazing of your bronchi irritated by your cough and you think about them, about your bronchi, you do it while I sleep. But I'm not altogether sleeping, I'm just faking it. We're no longer sleeping nor awake, isn't that right, Ximena? Yes, she answers me. Further over, in the cracks in the door, on the very tiniest edge one of the cells is sheltering, it's asleep or it's dead, it is seven stains, seven perforations that form or formed a cell. Seven. Ximena laughs, tells me a dirty joke, a gruesome and dirty joke that compromises the moral integrity of all the cells. I don't know how to laugh at her wit. Often Ximena will remember jokes or stories that are never simple and that end up revealing events you find reprehensible. But that's what Ximena's like, it's just what she's like, so expressive, so tall and expressive. I went to bed, Ximena tells me, with the whole of that cell, the cell with one-arm, remember?, I did it in every position, at any time. I slept with one of the leaders too, with a member of the central committee, no, no, I correct her, with the whole committee. And what about you?, she says to me, what about you? And you're furious, you're shaking, you want to kill us, Ximena and me. Right now we're alone, the three of us, for a few hours, later the shreds of the cells will start to surface jabbering their slogans and the usual complaints. For the moment, those cells are asleep, on their feet the way some animals do it. The three of us are on the bed, the bed I shared with the boy, taking care not to crush him, not to crush him, so that he would not die on me.

Whose is it?

You asked me at night, you did it so I couldn't see the intent in your face, you talked in the darkness and I understood that you didn't need an answer because what was essential to you was asking me the question and for my answer to end up letting you quit the room and go out. Whose is it? What a stupid question I want to reply, anyone's, well everyone's, what does it matter. But I give no answer at all, not a word, it's a recurring question, always. You lay there observing my cellular behaviour, the

154

movement of my hands. Ximena feigns outrage. As if not her, not her.

And here come all the cells, in groups that seem excessive or endless, they arrive diligently just when I'm so very tired, they're coming to take control of our bodies and to sound out our pains. Everything hurts. Everything. Our bones hurt and the purulent infection emanating from some of our organs. The cells move us and turn us over, they say we're dirty, sick, paralysed, that they need to bathe us, that relegated to the back rooms of each of the houses that still exist in the city (they are referring, of course, to the old buildings) we're contaminating them with our impossible odours. The cells shake us aggressively and alarmingly, they want to take my boy from me and they're looking for my last confession. The boy and I made up one cellular fabric, we are identical, a perfect human genome. Not human, no, never that.

Now you know, Ximena says to me: he killed you with a great blow to the head that destroyed your skull, then he broke your hands. You couldn't get up because you were no longer obeying even your own orders. He lied to Gómez, he told him you'd demanded too much ether, an ether he couldn't or didn't know how to monitor. Gómez wanted to believe him because he didn't know what to do, but in reality Gómez didn't believe a word. He knew he beat you to death. But he wasn't going to inform against a secret militant, never that, not Gómez. Ximena tells me this and she keeps repeating it to sow terrible discord between us. The old cells arrive, frozen or frightened or severely faulty. They all arrive and I almost don't recognise them, but there's no reason I should remember every one of them, right? The bed, our bed, the usual one, resembles a sub-proletarian hostel from another century, from another, a bed crammed full of cells. Get out of my bed, all of you, right now, get out, I say to them. Wake up, you say to me, be quiet. You want to convince me I'm having a nightmare, it's better, it's better. Ximena is at the foot of the bed and doesn't let you stretch your legs. You never managed to stretch your legs again, your broken legs that now give you a lot of pain, so much of it, because you can't even have the satisfaction of putting your legs however you fancy, a century or two with broken legs, who'd have thought it.

I need to get up from the bed, go to the kitchen, prepare the rice, put two bread rolls on the plate, just two. I need to return to the bedroom and run the comb over my broken, battered head, I need to invent some hands for myself because I shouldn't go out like this, I don't want to inform against you, that's not appropriate or necessary. I put on my coat. I look at the heap of cells that are already in an advanced state of deterioration, I pause at your mean little cells and they make me so very eager to say to you: get up, or say to you: revive yourself once and for all and let's go out with the boy, my own, the boy who is two, my beloved boy and let's take him to the hospital. We should take him because, after all, we have nothing left to lose.

CHARCO PRESS

Director & Editor: Carolina Orloff
Director: Samuel McDowell

www.charcopress.com

*Never Did the Fire* was published on
80gsm Munken Premium Cream paper.

The text was designed using Bembo 11.5 and ITC Galliard.

Printed in November 2021 by TJ Books
Padstow, Cornwall, PL28 8RW using responsibly
sourced paper and environmentally-friendly adhesive.

MIX
Paper from
responsible sources
FSC® C013056
FSC
www.fsc.org